This book belongs to

Maryam Bukhari

365
Stories
and
Rhymes

Original stories written by: Beth Shoshan, Beverley Gooding, Claire Freedman,
Gillian Rogerson, Lulu Frost, Mandy Archer, Rachael Duckett, Rachel Elliot.
Selected stories retold by Claire Sipi.

Cover illustrated by Jill Howarth.
Illustrated by: Ada Pianura, Alessandra Psacharopulo, Alison Brown, Ayesha Lopez,
Barroux, Beverley Gooding, Brenna Vaughan, Bruno Merz, Charlotte Cooke,
Chiara Fiorentino, Christine Tappin, Deborah Allwright, Dubravka Kolanovic, Emma Levey,
Erica-Jane Waters, Erin McGuire, Fiona Rose, Fran Brylewska, Gabriel Alborozo,
Gail Yerrill, Hannah George, Harriet Muncaster, Henry Fisher, Jacqueline East,
Julie Clay, Katy Hudson, Katya Longhi, Kirsten Richards, Kristina Swarner, Lisa Sheehan,
Livia Coloji, Lorena Alvarez, Loretta Schauer, Lorna Brown, Mar Ferrero, Maria Bogade,
Marilyn Faucher, Natalie Hinrichsen, Nicola Slater, Petra Brown, Rebecca Elliott,
Russell Julian, Stephen Gulbis, Valeria Do Campo, Victoria Assanelli.

Designed by Duck Egg Blue and Kathryn Davies
Edited by Grace Harvey and Becky Wilson
Production by Michaela Bartzsch

Every effort has been made to acknowledge the contributors to this book.
If we have made any errors, we will be pleased to rectify them in future editions.

This edition published by Parragon Books Ltd in 2016 and distributed by

Parragon Inc.
440 Park Avenue South, 13th Floor
New York, NY 10016
www.parragon.com

ISBN 978-1-4748-2096-7

Printed in China

365
Stories
and
Rhymes

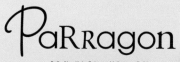

PaRRagon

Bath • New York • Cologne • Melbourne • Delhi
Hong Kong • Shenzhen • Singapore

Contents

The Little Mermaid

Far, far out to sea, where the water is crystal clear, lies a secret kingdom. Here a mer-king lived with his six mermaid daughters.

The youngest was a quiet girl, with a gentle heart. She dreamed of faraway adventures in the world above the sea.

"Once a mermaid is fifteen," said her grandmother, "she is allowed to swim up to the surface. Be patient, little one, your turn will come."

One by one, the little mermaid's sisters came of age, and visited the surface. They returned full of stories of all the things they had seen.

At last it was the turn of the little mermaid. She floated eagerly up toward the sea's surface.

When she finally pushed her face out through the salty swell, she saw a fine ship floating nearby. The people were throwing a party for the handsome prince on board.

The little mermaid couldn't take her eyes off the prince.

As she swam closer for a better look, a storm suddenly sprang up and tossed the ship about on the huge waves.

The little mermaid watched in horror as the prince was thrown into the churning sea. She dove down to rescue him. Holding him in her arms, the little mermaid swam to shore and gently pushed the unconscious prince onto the beach.

When she saw some people coming down the beach to help the prince, she leaped back into the waves and swam home.

From that moment on, the little mermaid could think of nothing but the prince and how she longed to be with him.

One day, when she couldn't bear it any longer, she visited the evil sea witch.

"I can give you a potion to make you human, but I will take your beautiful voice in return," cackled the witch. "If you fail to win the prince's love, you will melt into sea foam and be gone forever!"

The little mermaid loved the prince so much that she agreed.

She swam to the shore and drank the potion, then fell into a deep sleep. When she woke up she was lying in the prince's palace. She tried to speak, but her voice was lost forever, and she could only smile at her handsome rescuer.

The prince was intrigued by the silent stranger. He took her everywhere, and the little mermaid had never been happier.

Then, one day, the prince told her that he
was to be married, but that he loved another
girl, who had once rescued him from the sea.
Without her voice, the little mermaid couldn't
tell the prince that she was that girl.

On the day of the prince's wedding, the
prince walked with the little mermaid along
the beach. Suddenly, a huge wave crashed over
the prince and the little mermaid, washing
them out to sea. Without thinking, the little
mermaid dove beneath the churning waves
and grabbed the prince, taking him back to
the shore.

"You're the girl who saved me before!"
he cried.

The little mermaid smiled and nodded.

"I can't marry the princess. I love you," he
sighed. "Will you marry me?" And as he kissed
her, something magical happened. She could
feel her voice returning!

"Yes!" she cried out with joy.

The couple were married the very next
day. The little mermaid's dreams had come
true, but she never forgot her family, or
that she had once been a mermaid.

Hoppity Rabbit's Big Adventure

Hoppity Rabbit lived in a beautiful meadow at the edge of the woods. He spent his days happily running and jumping and hopping through the tall grass, chasing butterflies and playing hide-and-seek with his best friend, Boppity Rabbit.

On the other side of the meadow was a large stream. Hoppity loved to watch the fish darting about through the clear, flowing water, traveling on their journey toward the sea.

"I wonder what the sea is like?" Hoppity sighed, as he stared at the fish.

"Why don't we go on an adventure to find out?" said Boppity. "Look! The fish are swimming that way. If we follow the stream in the same direction, it should lead us to the sea."

Hoppity grinned. He'd never left the meadow or been on an adventure before.

"Let's pretend we're two fish racing to the sea!" Hoppity shouted, and dashed after Boppity along the grassy bank.

After a while, the grass stopped. A long, sandy beach stretched before them. The two little rabbits couldn't believe their eyes. The golden sand was covered with endless treasures of colored shells and pebbles, curling seaweed, and little scuttling crabs.

Hoppity grabbed Boppity's paw and turned to stare at the sea.

"It's even better than I imagined!" he cried, as the waves gently lapped at his feet. "Thank you, Boppity. This is the best adventure ever!"

I Had Two Pigeons

I had two pigeons, bright and gay,
They flew from me the other day:
What was the reason they did go?
I cannot tell, for I do not know.
Coo-oo, coo-oo!

The Groundhog

If the groundhog sees his shadow,
We will have six more weeks of winter.
If he doesn't see his shadow,
We will have an early spring.

The Little White Duck

There's a little white duck, "Quack!"
Sitting in the water.
A little white duck, "Quack!"
Doing what he oughter.
He took a bite of a lily pad,
Flapped his wings, and he said,
"I'm glad I'm a little white duck
Sitting in the water.
Quack, quack, quack!"

The Magpie

Magpie, magpie,
Flutter and flee,
Turn up your tail,
And good luck come to me.

If I Were a Bird

If I were a bird, I'd sing a song
And fly about the whole day long.
And when the night came, I'd go to rest
Up in my cozy little nest.

Haymaking

The maids in the meadow
Are making the hay.
The ducks in the river
Are swimming away.

Ollie's Adventure

One day, Ollie the dolphin was playing in the deep, bubbly ocean. His mom was nearby, but he was busy doing somersaults, twirls, and loops. Then, all of a sudden, Ollie was alone. He couldn't see his mom anywhere.

"Mom!" he called. "Where are you?" The ocean suddenly seemed very big.

Soon, Ollie saw a crab scuttling along the seabed.

"Will you help me find my mom?" Ollie asked.

The crab clicked his pincers. "I'm too busy to look for dolphins," he snapped, so Ollie swam on.

After a while, Ollie came to a big underwater cave. An octopus floated out toward him.

"Have you seen my mom?" Ollie asked.

The octopus shook his head.

"Ask the jellyfish," he said. But the glowing jellyfish just shrugged, then opened and closed like an umbrella.

"Oh dear," said Ollie. "How am I ever going to find my way home?"

Then, suddenly, Ollie remembered something.

"If you ever get lost, I will wait for you next to the big shipwreck," his mom had told him.

Ollie darted after the jellyfish. "Which way is the big shipwreck?" he asked.

This time, the jellyfish knew the answer. "I'll light the way!" she said.

As they passed the cave, Ollie called out to the octopus, "We're on the way to the shipwreck!"

"I know where that is!" boomed the octopus. He used his tentacles to point the way.

Even the crab helped lead Ollie to the big shipwreck. And there beside it was …

"Mom!" Ollie darted toward her, and they rubbed noses.

"I'm so happy you remembered our meeting place," said Ollie's mom.

"Me too," said Ollie. "And now that I know my way here, I will never get lost again!"

Alice's Vacation

Alice was so excited about going on vacation! She hopped up and down by the door while Mom checked the locks and Dad looked for his sandals.

"Please hurry up!" cried Alice.

It took hours to drive to the airport. Then they had to check in, line up, show their passports, and wait as the luggage was loaded onto the airplane.

"Too much waiting!" cried Alice.

On the plane, Alice talked to Mom and Dad until they fell asleep. Then she talked to herself. "I'm too excited to sleep!" she said.

When the plane landed, they had to wait for their luggage, line up, show their passports, and wait for a taxi. Alice gave a big, BIG yawn.

In the hotel room, Mom and Dad unpacked and changed into their swimsuits while Alice rested her eyes.

"Beach time!" said Mom. But Alice had fallen asleep!

Beach Penguin

Theo the penguin loved his snowy home. He loved jumping off icebergs and swimming races with his best friend Sophie. But one night, his iceberg home floated away into warmer water and melted. When Theo woke up, he was near a beach!

"This place is amazing!" he exclaimed, waddling onto the sand.

Theo sunbathed in a striped deck chair. He built a huge sandcastle. He rented a surfboard and rode the waves. He caught some tiny fish in the rock pools. He even had an ice cream!

Then, when his flippers were sandy and he was getting tired, he spotted a ship heading toward his home.

"Time to hitch a ride!" said Theo, diving into the warm water.

He couldn't wait to tell Sophie about his travels—and plan his next beach adventure!

In Lincoln Lane

I lost my mare in Lincoln Lane,
I'll never find her there again;
She lost a shoe, and then lost two,
And threw her rider in the drain.

Kindness

If I had a donkey that would not go,
Would I scold him? Oh, no, no.
I'd put him in the barn and give him some corn,
The best little donkey that ever was born.

The Old Woman's Three Cows

There was an old woman who had three cows,
Rosy and Colin and Dun.
Rosy and Colin were sold at the fair,
And Dun could not be found anywhere.
So there was an end of her three cows,
Rosy and Colin and Dun.

If Pigs Could Fly

If pigs could fly
High in the sky,
Where do you think they'd go?
Would they follow a plane
To France or Spain,
Or drift where the wind blows?

My Little Cow

I had a little cow,
Hey diddle, ho diddle!
I had a little cow, and I drove it to the stall;
Hey diddle, ho diddle! And there's my song all.

Grig's Pig

Grandpa Grig
Had a pig,
In a field of clover;
Piggy lied,
Grandpa cried,
And all the fun was over.

23

Adventure Balloon

Eloise raced across the hill, panting and giggling.

"You can't catch me!" she yelled.

Her little brother Hal was behind her, running as fast as he could. Scruffy, their dog, barked and yapped as he bounded along beside Hal.

Suddenly, they saw a big basket sitting at the top of the hill. A huge hot-air balloon was attached to it, bobbing around in the breeze.

"It's beautiful!" said Eloise. "Let's go for a ride!"

"Hurray! An adventure!" said Hal. "Come on, Scruffy. Let's go!"

Eloise hopped inside the basket, followed by Scruffy. Hal clambered in after them and then, magically, the balloon began to rise into the sky. They floated up among the fluffy white clouds. Birds fluttered around them, twittering with curiosity. The green hills and tall trees seemed small and far away. Scruffy barked and wagged his tail.

"Where shall we go?" Eloise called to the birds.

They cheeped even louder, but the children couldn't understand them. The balloon floated far over the land, and, soon, they saw a rainbow-colored tent in a green field.

"The circus!" Hal cried, clapping his hands. "I want to go to the circus!"

At once, the balloon floated down from the sky, heading toward the field.

As it got closer, clowns, jugglers, and dancers came out of the tent. "Come and join our show!" they called out.

As soon as the balloon landed, Eloise, Hal, and Scruffy raced inside the tent. It was lit by sparkling stars, and colorful balloons floated down to a huge crowd.

"Let the show begin!" cried a clown on stilts.

Scruffy did flips and somersaults on the back of a white horse, while Hal tiptoed across the tightrope.

Eloise stepped onto the circus swings, thinking of the birds that had flown around the balloon.

25

"I want to fly like the birds," she whispered.

Then she flew from swing to swing in the high roof of the tent, ever faster and higher. The crowd went wild.

Later, at the end of the show, the top of the circus tent opened like a lid. Everyone looked up. The hot-air balloon was floating above them.

"It's time to go!" Eloise told Hal and Scruffy.

They climbed into the basket and waved to the crowds and all the circus people below.

Then the balloon rose up into the clouds again. Eloise, Hal, and Scruffy clung to the basket tightly as they soared with the birds, bees, and butterflies.

Suddenly, the wind died down.

"Look!" said Eloise, peering over the edge of the basket. "We're back on the hill again."

Gently, the balloon bumped down onto the soft grass, and they all tumbled out. They lay on their backs, looking up at the blue sky.

"That was amazing," said Hal.

"WOOF!" said Scruffy.

"What an adventure!" said Eloise.

She laughed as the balloon seemed to give a little hop of excitement.

"See? The balloon thinks so too," she added with a giggle. "Come on, let's go home."

Pet Pal

Betsy felt sad and lonely. Her best friend in the world, Polly, had moved away.

"Why don't we go to the park?" suggested her mom. "Or you could read a book?" But nothing was fun without Polly.

Betsy's dad came home and gave her a hug.

"Don't look so sad," he said. "I've got a new friend for you." He opened a basket, and Betsy peeped inside.

"Meeow!" A sweet little kitten peered back at her.

But Betsy looked away. She didn't want a new friend. She wanted Polly!

The kitten clambered up onto the chair beside Betsy. It patted her hand with a soft paw, but Betsy pulled her hand away. So the kitten nudged her with its little nose. Its whiskers tickled Betsy's arm, and she couldn't help smiling.

"All right," she said. "Let's play."

Betsy made necklaces with colored beads and threads, and the kitten loved to pounce on them. Then, when Betsy painted a picture, the kitten added her own pretty paw prints to the scene

After lunch, the two played hide-and-seek in the garden. Then, just before tea time, Betsy read a book to her new friend.

Betsy didn't stop thinking about Polly, but she stopped feeling so sad. Instead, she thought about how much Polly would like the kitten.

After dinner, the kitten curled up on Betsy's lap. Betsy wrote a letter to Polly. She had lots to say! She told Polly all about the little kitten and the things they had done together. It was fun to remember their adventures.

"I still miss you very much," she wrote. "But I think I will enjoy writing letters to you. And my new kitten will make sure I have plenty to tell you!"

Vintery, Mintery

Vintery, mintery, cutery, corn,
Apple seed and apple thorn;
Wire, briar, limber lock,
Three geese in a flock.
One flew east, and one flew west,
And one flew over the cuckoo's nest.

Cuckoo, Cuckoo, What Do You Do?

Cuckoo, cuckoo, what do you do?
In April I open my bill;
In May I sing all day;
In June I change my tune;
In July away I fly;
In August away I must.

Three Ducks in a Brook

Look, look, look!
Three ducks in a brook.
One is white, and one is brown.
One is swimming upside down.
Look, look, look!
Three ducks in a brook.

Row, Row, Row Your Boat

Row, row, row your boat
Gently down the stream.
Merrily, merrily, merrily, merrily,
Life is but a dream.

One, Two, Three, Four, Five

One, two, three, four, five,
Once I caught a fish alive.
Six, seven, eight, nine, ten,
Then I let it go again.
Why did you let it go?
Because it bit my finger so.
Which finger did it bite?
This little finger on the right.

Sugarplum and the Butterfly

Sugarplum was always given the most important work. The Fairy Queen said it was because she was the kindest and most helpful of all the fairies.

"Sugarplum," said the Fairy Queen, one day. "I've got a very important job for you to do. I want you to make a rose-petal ball gown for my birthday ball next week."

"It will be my pleasure," said Sugarplum happily.

Sugarplum began to gather cobwebs for the thread, and rose petals for the dress. While she was collecting the thread, she found a butterfly caught in a cobweb.

"Oh, you poor thing," sighed Sugarplum.

Very carefully, she untangled the butterfly, but his wing was broken. Sugarplum laid the butterfly on a bed of feathers. She gathered some nectar from a special flower and fed him a drop at a time. Then she set about mending his wing with a magic spell.

After six days, the butterfly was better. He was very grateful. But now Sugarplum was behind with her work!

"Oh dear! I shall never finish the Fairy Queen's ball gown by tomorrow," she cried. "Whatever shall I do?"

The butterfly comforted her. "Don't worry, Sugarplum," he said. "We'll help you."

He gathered all his friends together. There were yellow, blue, red, and orange butterflies. He told them how Sugarplum had rescued him from the cobweb and helped mend his wing.

The butterflies gladly gathered up lots of rose petals and dropped them next to Sugarplum. Then the butterflies flew away to gather more cobwebs, while Sugarplum arranged all the petals. Back and forth went Sugarplum's hand with her needle and thread, making the finest cobweb stitches. Sugarplum added satin ribbons and bows. When she had finished, Sugarplum was very pleased with the ball gown.

"Dear friend," she said to the butterfly, "I couldn't have finished the dress without your help."

"And I could never have flown again without your kindness and help," said the butterfly.

And the Fairy Queen was delighted with her new ball gown!

The Best Zoo Ever!

Z oe the zookeeper had just finished doing her last rounds of the day to check on the animals. Normally at this time, the zoo would be noisy with happy squawks, growls, splashes, and toots. But not tonight. Silence had replaced the usual animal chatter.

"What's wrong?" Zoe asked the big gray elephant, as she passed his enclosure on her way to the main gates. "Why is everyone so quiet?"

"We're bored," trumpeted the elephant. "Nothing exciting ever happens here."

Zoe didn't want the animals to be unhappy. What could she do to cheer them up?

That night, as she lay in bed, Zoe suddenly had a great idea. She decided to call some of her friends in the morning to see if they could help her put it into action.

All of the following week, the zoo was noisy with the sound of hammering and sawing, digging, and drilling. The animals looked on curiously as Zoe and her friends rushed around, wearing hard hats and tool belts, and carrying planks of wood and plastic pipes.

At last, the project was finished. Zoe called all the animals together. They couldn't believe their eyes! There, in the middle of the zoo, was the most amazing adventure play area.

"I hope this will stop you from being bored," said Zoe. "I declare this zoo-tastic park open!"

And for the rest of that day the animals played hide-and-seek in the trees and bushes. They slithered down the slide and swung from the bars of the jungle gym.

That evening, as Zoe settled the animals back into their enclosures, she smiled at all their happy faces.

"Thank you so much, Zoe!" cried the big, gray elephant. "We had so much fun today. This really is the best zoo ever!"

The Wedding of Mrs. Fox

Mrs. Fox was feeling very sad because her husband had died.

"Don't be so sad," said her friend, Mrs. Cat. "You'll soon find someone else to marry." But Mrs. Fox wasn't so sure.

"I'll never find another husband as good as Mr. Fox," she sighed. "He had such a beautiful bushy tail and such a lovely pointed mouth."

The next day, Mrs. Cat knocked on Mrs. Fox's door.

"Here's Mr. Badger to see you," she said.

And in came Mr. Badger. Mrs. Fox could not deny that he had lovely black and white stripes, but he did not have a beautiful bushy tail or a lovely pointed mouth. So, when he asked Mrs. Fox to be his wife, she turned him down.

The following morning, Mrs. Cat knocked on her friend's door again. This time, she had brought Mr. Squirrel to see Mrs. Fox.

Mrs. Fox admired Mr. Squirrel's beautiful bushy tail, but he did not have a lovely pointed mouth. So when he begged her to marry him, Mrs. Fox said that she would rather not.

The following morning, Mrs. Cat knocked on Mrs. Fox's door yet again.

"Here's Mr. Mouse to see you," she said. And in came Mr. Mouse.

Mrs. Fox had to admit that he did have an attractive pointed mouth, but no beautiful bushy tail. So when he popped the question, Mrs. Fox was flattered, but still refused him.

A few days later, Mrs. Cat knocked on Mrs. Fox's door again.

"There's someone to see you," she said. And in came a handsome fox. He had a lovely pointed mouth and a beautiful bushy tail. The handsome fox visited Mrs. Fox every day … and soon they fell in love.

"Mrs. Fox, will you be my bride?" asked the handsome fox.

"Yes!" replied Mrs. Fox. And they lived happily ever after.

The Nutcracker

It was Christmas Eve, and Clara and her brother Fritz were very excited. That night, there was going to be a magnificent party at their house.

Fritz was busy playing with his toy soldiers, while Clara finished decorating their enormous tree with a beautiful fairy in a sugarplum-colored dress.

At last, the guests started arriving for the party.

"Look, there's Godfather Drosselmeyer!" said Fritz.

Their godfather was a famous toymaker. He hugged the children close, and then gave them their gifts.

Fritz eagerly unwrapped a mechanical gumball machine. For Clara, there was a wooden nutcracker in the shape of a soldier.

"I love him," Clara whispered. "Thank you, Godfather."

"But he's a soldier," said Fritz. "He should be mine."

Fritz tried to snatch the Nutcracker away from her. He pulled and Clara tugged, and then … CRACK!

The Nutcracker's leg snapped off!

"I can fix him, Clara," said their godfather gently. He pulled a little tool pouch from his pocket and quickly mended the Nutcracker.

"Oh, thank you," cried Clara. She placed the Nutcracker carefully under the Christmas tree and went to join the party.

Finally, the last dance was danced and the guests had said their goodbyes. The family went to bed and the house was dark and quiet.

BONG! BONG!

Clara awoke to hear the clock striking midnight. She suddenly remembered she'd left the Nutcracker under the tree, so she tiptoed downstairs. As she bent down to pick him up, the tree suddenly started to grow! Or was it that Clara was shrinking?

"What's happening?" she cried.

"Don't be afraid," said a kind voice.

Clara turned around. Her Nutcracker had come alive! Behind him, Fritz's soldiers were sitting up in their toybox.

Before Clara could speak, she heard a scurrying sound, and an army of mice poured into the room, led by a giant Mouse King with a golden crown.

"Attack!" he squeaked.

"To battle!" ordered the Nutcracker, and Fritz's soldiers marched boldly toward the attacking mice.

Suddenly, Clara saw the Mouse King spring at the Nutcracker. She snatched off her slipper and hurled it at the Mouse King. He fell to the ground, and his crown tumbled from his head.

With their leader defeated, the mice scurried away in fear.

The Nutcracker picked up Clara's slipper.

"I owe you my life, Clara," he said. "You broke the spell that was put on me long ago by a wicked Mouse Queen."

Clara gasped—the Nutcracker had been transformed into a handsome prince!

"Come," said the prince, as he helped Clara into a magical sleigh. "I'll take you on a wonderful adventure."

The walls of the sitting room seemed to fade away, and a sleigh drew up. They climbed aboard, and it flew high into the starry sky.

"Where are we?" gasped Clara.

"This is the Kingdom of Sweets," said the prince.

Gently, the sleigh landed beside a magnificent marzipan palace.

"Look," said the prince, waving to a fairy by the gate. "It's the Sugarplum Fairy!"

"Prince Nutcracker!" cried the fairy. "You are home at last!"

"This is Princess Clara," said the prince. "She saved my life and broke the Mouse Queen's spell."

The Sugarplum Fairy hugged Clara. "Let's celebrate!" she said.

Inside the palace, Clara and the prince feasted on delicious cakes and sweets. They watched in wonder as the Sugarplum Fairy twirled around the room to the beautiful music.

Clara's eyelids began to droop and the sound of the music became fainter and fainter ….

When Clara woke up on Christmas morning, she found herself curled up under the Christmas tree next to the Nutcracker.

"I've had the most wonderful adventure," sighed Clara, and she told her parents all about it.

"It was just a dream, darling," said her mother.

Clara gazed up at the sugarplum-colored fairy on top of the tree. Then she looked at the wooden Nutcracker in her hands.

"Perhaps it was," she said. But then, Clara noticed something glinting on the carpet, and a smile spread across her face.

It was a tiny golden crown.

The Old Woman and the Fat Hen

There was once an old woman who kept a hen that laid one egg every morning without fail. The eggs were large and delicious, and the old woman was able to sell them for a very good price at market.

"If my hen would lay two eggs every day," she said to herself, "I would be able to earn twice as much money!"

So, every evening, the old woman fed the hen twice as much food.

Each day, the old woman went to the henhouse expecting to find two eggs, but there was still only one—and the hen was getting fatter and fatter.

One morning, the woman looked in the nest box, and there were no eggs at all. There were none the next day, nor any the day after that. All the extra food had made the hen so fat and contented that she had become lazy and had given up laying eggs altogether!

And the moral of the story is: Things don't always work out as planned.

The Mice Come Up with a Plan

Once there was a large family of mice who lived in a big old house. Everything would have been perfect, except for one thing—the cat who lived there too. Each time the mice crept into the kitchen to nibble a few crumbs, the cat would pounce and chase them under the floorboards.

"If we don't come up with a plan soon, we'll starve," cried Grandfather Mouse.

But the mice couldn't agree on a single idea. Finally, the youngest mouse had a brainstorm.

"We could put a bell on the cat's collar so we can hear him coming," he suggested.

All the mice thought this was an excellent plan.

Then Grandfather Mouse stood up.

"You are a very smart young fellow to come up with such an idea," he said. "But, tell me, who is going to be brave enough to put the bell on the cat's collar?"

And the moral of the story is: It is sometimes easy to think of a clever plan, but it can be much more difficult to carry it out.

Mermaid's Treasure

One morning, Pearl the mermaid was playing around a reef when she spotted a large sea chest among the coral. She swam closer.

"It must have fallen out of a ship," she exclaimed. "I wonder what's inside!"

But when she tried to lift the lid, she found that it was locked.

"Oh, bother," Pearl muttered. "Now I want to look inside even more!"

She tried to force the lid open with a clam shell, but it wouldn't budge. So she asked her biggest, strongest friends for help.

Shark tried to bite a hole in it. Octopus wrapped his tentacles around the chest and tried to squeeze it open. Whale tried crushing it with his weight.

"It's no use," sighed Pearl. "We'll never get it open."

"May I try?" said a squeaky voice in her ear.

Pearl turned and saw a tiny shrimp, no bigger than her fingernail. She smiled at him. How could someone so small open the chest?

"Of course you may," she said politely.

The little shrimp wriggled through the keyhole. Pearl, Shark, Octopus, and Whale watched as he reached into the lock with his spindly legs. Then there was a loud click, and the chest unlocked.

The shrimp swam out, looking very pleased with himself.

"Well done!" cried Pearl.

Slowly, she lifted the lid. The chest was full of men's clothes! Pearl sat back and laughed loudly.

"Some poor sailor has lost his luggage," she chuckled. "I suppose it would be treasure to him!"

She looked at her friends and laughed again.

"Don't look so disappointed," she went on. "We may not have gold or jewels, but we've made a very clever friend."

And the little pink shrimp blushed bright red!

Magpie's Nest

Long ago, the other birds wanted to know how Magpie built the best nests.

"Gather round, and I will teach you," cried Magpie.

First of all, she took some mud and made a round bowl shape.

"Ah, so that's how it's done," squawked Thrush, flying away. And, today, that is how thrushes build their nests.

Next, Magpie twined some twigs around the mud.

"Now I know all about it," tweeted Sparrow, and off he flew. And that's how sparrows make their nests to this very day.

Then, Magpie lined the nest with feathers.

"Oh, that suits me," chirped Starling, and off she went. And that's why starlings have very comfortable nests.

At each step, another bird flew away. By the time Magpie got to the last stage, all the birds had gone.

Magpie laughed. "I will never show them again!"

And that is why birds all build their nests differently.

I Had a Little Nut Tree

I had a little nut tree, nothing would it bear,
But a silver nutmeg, and a golden pear;
The King of Spain's daughter came to visit me,
And all for the sake of my little nut tree.

The Apple Tree

Here is the tree with leaves so green.
Here are the apples that hang between.
When the wind blows, the apples fall.
Here is a basket to gather them all.

The Cherry Tree

Once I found a cherry stone,
I put it in the ground,
And when I came to look at it,
A tiny shoot I found.

The shoot grew up and up each day,
And soon became a tree.
I picked the rosy cherries then,
And ate them with my tea.

The Sparkly Princess and the Pea

Once upon a time, there lived the most sparkle-tastic princess EVER! Her name was Glitterbelle.

Glitterbelle loved anything glittery, shimmery, and purple. She also loved playing with her friends and climbing trees.

But there was something that Glitterbelle definitely did *not* love, and that was PEAS! She thought they were squishy, gross, and very … green.

"How do you know you don't like peas if you won't even try them?" asked King Alfie, one dinnertime. "We love them. In fact, we owe our kingdom to peas."

"It's how your great-great-great-great-grandpapa found your great-great-great-great-grandmama," added Queen Lizzie. "Remember the famous fairy tale?"

"Yes, I know," said Glitterbelle, with a sigh. "It's the one where great-great-great-great-grandmama had to prove to everyone she was a REAL princess by feeling *one* tiny pea under twenty mattresses."

"That's it," grinned King Alfie. "And we've still got that very same pea. It'll be yours some day!"

Glitterbelle looked at the dried-up pea, proudly sitting in a dusty glass case. "Yuck!" she groaned.

Just then, Glitterbelle's best friends Dazzlina, the witch, and Angel, the ballerina, came around to play at the palace. Sighing, Glitterbelle told her friends how much she hated peas.

"I must be the first princess EVER not to like them!" she said. "Maybe I'm not *really* a princess after all."

"Well, you do like climbing trees," said Angel thoughtfully.

"And racing around on your scooter," added Dazzlina. "They're not *very* princessy things to do."

"I knew it!" cried Glitterbelle. "I *am* different than fairy-tale princesses."

"We're only teasing you," laughed Dazzlina.

"We love you whether you're a fairy-tale princess or a scruffy, tree-climbing one," added Angel with a smile.

"Thanks," replied Glitterbelle. "But I don't feel like *any* kind of princess right now."

After her friends had left, Glitterbelle was still feeling sad.

"What's wrong?" asked Queen Lizzie at bath time.

"I'm not a real princess," cried Glitterbelle. "I don't act like one *or* look like one. I'm too ME to be a princess!"

"Oh, Glitterbelle," said Queen Lizzie, "you're a real princess just by being *you!*" She hugged her daughter. "It will all seem better in the morning, I promise."

After her bath, Glitterbelle went downstairs to drink some hot cocoa. Meanwhile, Queen Lizzie had an idea. She could prove to Glitterbelle that she really was a princess!

Smiling, the queen popped something small, round, and green under the mattress on Glitterbelle's bed.

That night, Glitterbelle tossed and turned— she barely slept a wink! The next morning, Glitterbelle woke up, aching all over.

As she climbed out of bed, a small green pea rolled out from under her mattress. The princess picked it up and knew at once why she hadn't been able to sleep.

The tiny pea proved that Glitterbelle was a fairy-tale princess after all, just like in the famous story.

"Mom! Dad!" Glitterbelle shouted, racing downstairs.
"Look! This LOVELY pea proves that I'm a real princess."

"We always knew you were," smiled the queen. "As well as being our special Glitterbelle princess, of course."

Glitterbelle beamed at her mom, then looked at the pea. "Maybe peas aren't so bad after all," she said.

The king and queen laughed.

"I think we should have a party to celebrate," said the king.

And all of Glitterbelle's friends and family were invited.

Later, when everyone sat down to a tasty banquet, Glitterbelle spotted a green cake … It had been made with a special ingredient—peas! Glitterbelle ate her slice, and smiled.

"This pea-green cake is delicious!" she said.

"You're a REAL fairy-tale princess now," giggled Dazzlina.

"Of the Glitterbelle kind!" added Angel.

Elsie's Airplane

Elsie was a pilot. Her little airplane was very old and quite slow, but Elsie didn't care. She loved flying it up into the bright blue sky.

One sunny day, Elsie hurried to the airfield where her little airplane lived. She and her friends were going to have a race in their different kinds of flying machine. One friend flew an airliner, another had a seaplane, the third had a rocket, and the last one had a jet. Each of them thought that they would be the fastest.

"Your slow, old airplane will come last," her friends said. But Elsie felt sure that her little airplane could do anything.

Elsie filled the fuel tanks and climbed into the cockpit. The five flying machines took off together, but they didn't stay together for long. The jet zoomed ahead. The airliner climbed high into the sky, and the rocket zigzagged around as if it were playing tag. Even the seaplane was going faster than Elsie.

"Don't worry," said Elsie, patting her little airplane. "I believe in you."

Suddenly, Elsie saw the airliner turn around and head back to the airfield.

"I forgot to fill up with fuel," said the pilot into his crackly radio.

Then the jet zoomed off in the wrong direction. Elsie tried to tell him, but he was going too fast to listen.

The rocket flew higher and higher … and ended up in space!

"Only us left now!" said the pilot of the seaplane.

But just then, the pilot saw a lake and couldn't resist practicing a water landing.

With a cheer, Elsie guided her little airplane over the finish line and won the race.

"We did it!" she cried. "Three cheers for the oldest, best little airplane in the world!"

Jackanory

I'll tell you a story
Of Jackanory,
And now my story's begun;
I'll tell you another
Of Jack and his brother,
And now my story's done.

Three Wise Men of Gotham

Three wise men of Gotham
Went to sea in a bowl:
And if the bowl had been stronger,
My song would have been longer.

Little Tommy Tittlemouse

Little Tommy Tittlemouse,
Lived in a little house;
He caught fishes
In other men's ditches.

Aiken Drum

There was a man lived in the moon,
Lived in the moon, lived in the moon.
There was a man lived in the moon,
And his name was Aiken Drum.

Harry Parry

O rare Harry Parry,
When will you marry?
When apples and pears are ripe.
I'll come to your wedding,
Without any bidding,
And dance and sing all the night.

Lucy Locket

Lucy Locket lost her pocket,
Kitty Fisher found it.
Not a penny was there in it,
Only ribbon around it.

Goldilocks and the
Three Bears

Once upon a time, there was a little girl named
Goldilocks who had beautiful golden hair. She lived
in a little cottage right at the edge of the forest.

One morning, before breakfast, Goldilocks skipped in to the
forest to play. She soon strayed far from home and began to
feel hungry.

Just as she was thinking about going home, a delicious smell
wafted through the woods. She followed it all the way to a
little cottage.

"I wonder who lives here?" thought Goldilocks. She knocked
on the door, but there was no answer.

As Goldilocks pushed gently on the door, it swung open, and
Goldilocks stepped inside.

The delicious smell was coming from three bowls of steaming porridge on a table. There was a great big bowl, a middle-sized bowl, and a teeny-tiny bowl.

Goldilocks was so hungry, she tried the porridge in the biggest bowl first. "Ooh! Too hot," she cried.

Next, she tasted the porridge in the middle-sized bowl. "Yuck! Too cold," she spluttered.

So Goldilocks tried the porridge in the teeny-tiny bowl. "Yum," she said. "Just right." And she ate it all up.

Goldilocks saw three comfy chairs by the fire. There was a great big chair, a middle-sized chair, and a teeny-tiny chair.

"Just the place for a nap," yawned Goldilocks sleepily.

She tried to scramble onto the biggest chair. "Too high up!" she gasped, sliding to the ground.

Next, Goldilocks tried the middle-sized chair, but she sank into the cushions. "Too squishy!" she grumbled.

So Goldilocks tried the teeny-tiny chair. "Just right!" she sighed, settling down.

But Goldilocks was full of porridge and too heavy for the teeny-tiny chair. It squeaked and creaked. Creaked and cracked.

Then... CRASH!

It broke into teeny-tiny pieces and Goldilocks fell to the floor.

"Ouch!" she said.

Goldilocks climbed up the stairs. At the top, she found
a bedroom with three beds. There was a great big bed, a
middle-sized bed, and a teeny-tiny bed.

"I'll just lie down for a while," yawned Goldilocks.

So she clambered onto the biggest bed. "Too hard,"
she grumbled.

Then she lay down on the middle-sized bed. "Too soft!"
she mumbled.

So she snuggled down in the teeny-tiny bed. "Just right,"
she sighed, and fell fast asleep.

Meanwhile, a great big daddy bear, a
middle-sized mommy bear, and a teeny-tiny baby
bear returned home from their walk in the woods.

"The porridge should be cool enough to eat now,"
said Mommy Bear.

So the three bears went inside their cottage
for breakfast.

"Someone's been eating my porridge," growled
Daddy Bear, looking in his bowl.

"Someone's been eating my porridge,"
gasped Mommy Bear, looking in her bowl.

"Someone's been eating my porridge,"
squeaked Baby Bear, "and they've eaten it
all up!"

Then Daddy Bear went over to his chair.

"Someone's been sitting in my chair,"
he roared. "There's a golden hair on it!"

"Someone's been sitting in my chair," growled Mommy Bear. "The cushions are all squashed."

"Someone's been sitting in my chair," cried Baby Bear, "and they've broken it!"

The three bears stamped upstairs.

Daddy Bear looked at his crumpled bed covers.

"Someone's been sleeping in my bed!" he grumbled.

Mommy Bear looked at the jumbled pillows on her bed.

"Someone's been sleeping in my bed!" she said.

Baby Bear padded over to his bed.

"Someone's been sleeping in my bed," he cried, "and they're still there!"

At that moment, Goldilocks woke up. When she saw the three bears, she leaped out of bed, ran down the stairs, through the door, into the woods, and all the way home! And she never visited the house of the three bears ever again.

The Dinosaur Marching Band

One, two, three, four! Keep it up, two, three, four!
The jungle rumbles and the ground shakes.
CRASH! THUMP! What's that sound?

Oh, look! It's the dinosaur marching band, and they're coming this way! Crashing, stomping, singing, and playing their loud music as they sway through the trees.

STOMP! STOMP! TOOT! TOOT! BANG! BANG!

What an impressive noise they make!

Tommy T. Rex is at the head of the line. He leads his fellow musical marchers, tooting loudly on his golden trumpet, the melody floating on the air.

Following closely behind is Daisy Diplodocus. With a steady beat on her jungle drums, she sways her long neck and stamps her large feet, keeping the rhythm for the rest of the band.

Susie Stegosaurus sings her sweet, soulful song, hitting the high notes perfectly. LA, LA, LA, LA, LA!

Then there's Terry Pterodactyl, flying above his marching friends. He whistles the melody with Tommy's crisp trumpet notes, while Arthur Ankylosaurus hammers a bass beat on the ground in time with Daisy's drums.

And, last but not least, Trixie Triceratops stomps along at the back of the line, keeping time as she counts: "One, two, three, four! Keep it up, two, three, four!" She shouts out the numbers with a noisy ROAR!

STOMP! STOMP! TOOT! TOOT! BANG! BANG!

It's the wonderful musical dinosaur marching band … and they're coming your way.

Two Little Dickie Birds

Two little dickie birds sitting on a wall,
One named Peter, one named Paul.
Fly away Peter, fly away Paul.
Come back Peter, come back Paul.

Ten Green Bottles

Ten green bottles standing on the wall,
Ten green bottles standing on the wall,
And if one green bottle should accidentally fall,
There'd be nine green bottles standing on the wall.

You can keep counting down until there are no more bottles!

Magic Seed

I found a tiny little seed and planted it outside.
Almost at once it started to grow up, tall and wide.
It sprouted leaves from everywhere, and soon became quite big.
I'm not sure what it is yet—apples, pears, or figs?
No matter how it turns out, I know that it will be
My own completely special something-or-other tree!

One, Two, Buckle My Shoe

One, two, buckle my shoe,
Three, four, knock at the door,
Five, six, pick up sticks,
Seven, eight, lay them straight,
Nine, ten, a big fat hen,
Eleven, twelve, dig and delve,
Thirteen, fourteen, maids a-courting,
Fifteen, sixteen, maids in the kitchen,
Seventeen, eighteen, maids in waiting,
Nineteen, twenty, my plate's empty!

One Potato, Two Potato

One potato, two potato,
Three potato, four.
Five potato, six potato,
Seven potato,
MORE!

Eeny, Meeny

Eeny, meeny, miney, mo,
Catch a tiger by the toe,
If he hollers, let him go,
Eeny, meeny, miney, mo.

How the Tortoise Got His Cracked Shell

Once upon a time, there lived a tortoise. He was very sly, and the other animals didn't like him.

One day, all the birds were invited to a party in the sky. Tortoise wanted to go too, so he came up with a cunning plan. He told the birds that they would need a leader to do all the talking when they arrived at the party.

"I would make the best leader," he said, "because I am so good at talking!"

Although the birds didn't like Tortoise, they agreed that he was indeed very good at talking. Each bird gave one feather to Tortoise. He stuck them on his shell so that he could fly up to the sky with them.

Before they left, Tortoise told the birds that they would all need to choose a name, so they could introduce themselves at the party.

"My name will be 'All of You,'" he said.

When they arrived at the party and the food was brought out, Tortoise asked their hostess, "Whose food is this?"

The hostess replied, "This food is for all of you."

Tortoise turned to the birds.

"This food is for me. Perhaps they will bring out your food later?" And he ate all the food.

The birds didn't get anything to eat. They were very angry, and took back all their feathers from Tortoise's shell.

Tortoise couldn't fly home without the feathers. He begged the birds to take a message to his wife. Finally, Parrot agreed.

"Tell my wife to lay out pillows so that I will have a soft landing when I jump from the sky."

However, when Parrot saw Tortoise's wife, he told her to lay out all the sharpest things she could find.

At a signal from Parrot, Tortoise jumped.

Down he fell, and then CRACK! went his hard shell!

Afterwards, Tortoise's wife took him to the doctor. The doctor was able to put Tortoise's shell back together, but it was never smooth again.

And that's why all tortoises have cracked shells.

The Frog Prince

Long ago, a princess lived with her father in a palace surrounded by woods.

When it was hot outside, the princess would walk into the shade of the forest and sit by a pond. There she would play with her favorite toy, a golden ball.

One day, the ball slipped from her hand and fell to the bottom of the pond. "My beautiful golden ball," she sobbed.

An ugly, speckled frog popped his head out of the water. "Why are you crying?" he croaked.

"I've dropped my precious golden ball into the water," she cried.

"What will you give me if I get it for you?" asked the frog.

"You may have my jewels," sobbed the unhappy princess.

"I don't need those," said the frog. "If you promise to care for me and be my friend, let me share food from your plate and sleep on your pillow, then I will bring back your golden ball."

"I promise," said the princess, but she thought to herself, "He's only a silly old frog. I won't do any of those things."

When the frog returned with the ball, she snatched it from him and ran back to the palace.

That evening, the princess was having dinner with her father when there was a knock on the door.

When the princess opened the door, she was horrified to find the frog sitting there. She slammed the door and hurried back to the table.

"Who was that?" asked the king.

"Oh, just a frog," replied the princess.

"What does a frog want with you?" asked the puzzled king.

The princess told her father about the promise she had made.

"Princesses always keep their promises," insisted the king. "Let the frog in and make him welcome."

As soon as the frog hopped through the door he asked to be lifted up onto the princess's plate. When the frog saw the look of disgust on the princess's face, he sang:

"Princess, princess, fair and sweet, you made a special vow
To be my friend and share your food, so don't forget it now."

The king was annoyed to see his daughter acting so rudely. "This frog helped you," he said. "And now you must keep your promise to him."

For the rest of the day, the frog followed the princess everywhere she went. She hoped that he would go back to his pond when it was time for bed, but when darkness fell, the frog yawned and said, "I am tired. Take me to your room and let me sleep on your pillow."

The princess was horrified. "No, I won't!" she said rudely. "Go back to your pond and leave me alone!"

The patient frog sang:

"Princess, princess, fair and sweet, you made a special vow
To be my friend and share your food, so don't forget it now."

Reluctantly, the princess took the frog to her room. She couldn't bear the thought of sleeping next to him, so she put him on the floor. Then she climbed into her bed and went to sleep.

After a while, the frog jumped up onto the bed. "It's drafty on the floor. Let me sleep on your pillow," he said.

The sleepy princess felt more annoyed than ever. She picked up the frog and hurled him across the room. But when she saw him lying dazed and helpless on the floor, she was suddenly filled with pity.

"Oh, you poor darling!" she cried, and she picked him up and kissed him.

Suddenly, the frog transformed into a handsome young prince.

"Sweet princess," he cried. "I was bewitched, and your tender kiss has broken the curse!"

The prince and princess soon fell in love and were married. They often walked in the shady forest together and sat by the pond, tossing the golden ball back and forth, and smiling at how they met.

The Naughty Little Rabbits

Once upon a time, three naughty little rabbits lived with their mama in a cozy hillside burrow.

One day, Mama said, "You're getting so big! Come and help me make your sleeping dens bigger."

The naughty little rabbits didn't want to help Mama. "We want to play outside!" they cried.

"First, there is work to do," their mama said.

But the naughty little rabbits scampered off to the meadow, leaving their poor mama behind.

"I wish we had someone to play with," said the first little rabbit, looking around for some excitement.

"Why don't you play with me?" cried a squirrel. "Just do what I do, and we'll have some fun."

Then the squirrel scampered up a tree and started throwing acorns, which rained down upon the naughty little rabbits.

"Ow!" cried the little rabbits, and they ran away.

"I wish we had something to eat," said the second little rabbit, growing hungry after all that running.

"Why don't you have lunch with me?" croaked a little frog. "Just do what I do. Close your eyes and put out your tongues, and you'll catch a yummy fly."

"Yuck! We don't eat flies!" spluttered the little rabbits, pulling their tongues back in and hopping away.

"I wish we could have a cozy nap," said the third little rabbit, tired after so much hopping around.

But before they could curl up, it started to rain. The little rabbits didn't like the rain, and they ran until they reached home.

"We're so sorry, Mama!" cried the little rabbits, as she hugged them close. "Can we help you with the work now?"

"There will be plenty of work for you to do another day," said their mama. "Come and eat your supper, and promise me you won't run off again."

The hungry, sleepy little rabbits ate their supper. Then they crawled into their sleeping dens.

And guess what? Someone had made each one a little bit bigger. Now, who do you think had done that?

Butterfly

I'm a little butterfly
Born in a bower,
Flying, fluttering, gliding,
Resting on a flower.

Frisky Lamb

A frisky lamb
And a frisky child
Playing their pranks
In a cowslip meadow:
The sky all blue
And the air all mild
And the fields all sun
And the lanes half-shadow.

Mousie

Mousie comes a-creeping, creeping.
Mousie comes a-peeping, peeping.
Mousie says, "I'd like to stay,
but I haven't time today."
Mousie pops into his hole
And says, "Achoo! I've caught a cold!"

Little Cottage

Little cottage in the wood,
Little old man by the window stood,
Saw a rabbit running by,
Knocking at the door.
"Help me! Help me! Help me!" he said,
"Before the huntsman shoots me dead."
"Come little rabbit, come inside,
Safe with me abide."

To the Snail

Snail, snail, put out
your horns,
And I will give you bread
and barley corns.

A Frog He Would a-Wooing Go

A frog he would a-wooing go,
Heigh ho! says Rowley,
Whether his mother would let him or no,
With a rowley, powley, gammon and spinach,
Heigh ho! says Anthony Rowley.

The Enchanted Shell

Anna lived in a big, white house by the sea. She loved to watch the sun go down behind the waves and listen to the splashing of the surf.

One evening, she was walking along the beach when she saw a pearly pink shell lying on the sand.

"How pretty!" she said, picking up the shell. Suddenly, the shell started to sparkle. Then it rose into the air and flew into the sea, where it grew bigger and bigger, until it was the size of a small boat!

Anna climbed into the shell, and it took her farther and farther out to sea.

The stars came out, and moonlight danced on the water. Fish in all the colors of the rainbow swirled around the shell, making it spin slowly. A purple octopus peeped over the side of the shell and smiled at Anna.

From beneath the water, music rose up. It was the most wonderful music that Anna had ever heard. Then a beautiful mermaid appeared.

"My sisters and I make music every night," said the mermaid. "The octopus will look after your boat. Come and play!"

Anna slipped into the water, and the mermaid led her to a glimmering blue-green palace under the sea. Mermaids danced around Anna, their tails twinkling.

Anna stayed with the mermaids until the stars disappeared and the sun came up. It was time to leave. Anna swam to the boat, and it carried her back to the beach by her home.

Walking home, Anna held tightly to the little shell. She knew that more adventures would find her whenever she visited the beach with the special shell in the moonlight!

Small World

Elizabeth and Jamie were best friends, and they loved playing together in the woods behind their homes.

One day, when they were in Jamie's yard, Jamie saw a little grasshopper on the sidewalk outside. He picked him up with gentle hands.

"You might get stepped on if you stay there," Jamie told him. "We'll help you. We know how it feels to be small."

So Jamie and Elizabeth put the little grasshopper on some grass next to the sidewalk.

"Thank you," said the grasshopper. "You are very kind."

Jamie couldn't believe his ears. His mouth fell open in amazement.

"You can talk!" he exclaimed.

"All animals can talk," said the grasshopper. "We just don't choose to talk to humans very often. Would you like to come to the woods with me? I will take you to the Land of Animals. No human has ever visited it before!"

"We'd love to," said Elizabeth.

The grasshopper jumped ahead of them, and they ran down the path behind him, giggling as they chased the little green creature into the woods.

They ran and jumped over ferns and logs, until the grasshopper stopped beside a small green leaf. It had a hole in the middle of it. The grasshopper tapped the leaf with one of his wings, and the leaf grew until the hole was the size of a door. The grasshopper turned and smiled at them.

"Welcome to my home!" he said.

He hopped through the hole, and the children followed him.

Everything was different through the hole. The sky was bluer. The grass was greener. Even the sun shone a little more brightly. Best of all, everywhere the children looked, they saw animals. Everyone was playing happily. Butterflies danced together, making beautiful patterns and shapes with their wings. Bunnies hopped around them, and birds landed on their shoulders, singing their merriest songs.

"Look at the ladybugs!" cried Elizabeth. They were looping the loop and twisting and diving through the air.

Tiny brown bunny rabbits hopped around the trees, playing catch and hide-and-seek. When they saw the children, they stopped and waved their paws.

"Come and play with us!" they called.

Elizabeth and Jamie could hardly wait! They followed the rabbits as they bounded around the trees, and ran deeper into the Land of Animals.

The children hid among flowering bushes, and the rabbits looked for them, thumping their big feet in delight when they won.

Elizabeth and Jamie made friends with speckled deer, and climbed trees with the squirrels to look for nuts. Finally, the light faded, and owls peered out from trees with sleepy eyes.

"Time to go home," they hooted. "The grasshopper will be waiting for you."

Elizabeth and Jamie hurried back to the leaf with the big hole in it. The grasshopper was there, right beside the magical leaf.

"Did you have a good time?" he asked.

"It's been the most amazing day ever," said Elizabeth. "We've loved every moment."

"And we've loved having you visit the Land of Animals," the grasshopper replied. "You are very special. Not many humans remember how it feels to be small."

"We will never forget," said Jamie as they stepped back through the magical leaf door. "We promise!"

Coffee and Tea

Molly, my sister, and I fell out,
And what do you think it was all about?
She loved coffee and I loved tea,
And that was the reason we couldn't agree.

Polly, Put the Kettle On

Polly, put the kettle on,
Polly, put the kettle on,
Polly, put the kettle on,
We'll all have tea.

Sukey, take it off again,
Sukey, take it off again,
Sukey, take it off again,
They've all gone away.

I'm a Little Teapot

I'm a little teapot, short and stout,
Here's my handle, here's my spout.
When I get my steam up, hear me shout,
Tip me over, and pour me out.

Sippity Sup, Sippity Sup

Sippity sup, sippity sup,
Bread and milk from a china cup.
Bread and milk from a bright silver spoon
Made of a piece of the bright silver moon.
Sippity sup, sippity sup,
Sippity, sippity sup.

Star Light, Star Bright

Star light, star bright,
The first star I see tonight;
I wish I may, I wish I might,
Have the wish I make tonight.

Hey Diddle Diddle

Hey diddle diddle,
The cat and the fiddle,
The cow jumped over the moon.
The little dog laughed to see such fun,
And the dish ran away with the spoon!

Princess Bea's Wish

Princess Bea didn't like getting messy. She would rather play in her bedroom, where everything was neat and tidy, than go outside and get muddy.

Then, on Bea's birthday, her fairy godmother gave her three magic wishes.

"Thank you!" Princess Bea said. "My first two wishes are a dollhouse and a toy puppy."

Bea's fairy godmother waved her wand and, with a tinkle of silver bells, the new toys magically appeared.

Bea started playing with them, but they weren't as much fun as she had hoped.

"I'm bored playing indoors," she thought.

So she went for a ride in her carriage. Soon she saw the village children sitting by the stream, looking sad. Bea stopped the carriage and got out.

"What's wrong?" she asked them.

"The rope swing over the stream has broken," said one of the children. "We've got nothing to play on."

Bea thought hard. She had lots of toys. She didn't really need her third wish.

"I wish for the rope swing to be repaired," she whispered.

Suddenly, there was a magical flash and lots of rope swings appeared over the river. The children squealed with delight.

"Come and play with us!" they called to Bea.

Bea thought it might be fun, so she did.

Later, when the princess went home, her dress was torn, her knees were muddy, and her hair was full of brambles. She had even lost one of her shoes!

"What a messy princess!" said her fairy godmother, smiling. "Did you have a good time?"

"Yes, thank you," said Bea. "Today was the best birthday ever! I had so much fun with my new friends, I forgot all about getting messy."

Jade and the Jewels

Jade was the prettiest mermaid in the lagoon. Her jet-black hair reached right down to the tip of her swishy, fishy tail. Her eyes were as green as emeralds, and her skin was as white as the whitest pearl. And she knew it!

"That Jade thinks too much of herself!" the other mermaids would say. "One of these days she'll be sorry."

Only one creature was fond of Jade. Gentle the giant turtle followed her wherever she went. But Jade didn't notice Gentle. She lived in her own world, spending all her time combing her hair and looking in the mirror.

One day, Jade overheard the other mermaids talking about a pirate ship that had sunk to the bottom of the ocean. On board was a treasure chest filled with precious jewels.

"But no one dares take the jewels," whispered the mermaids, "because the pirate ship is cursed!"

"I'm going to find that pirate ship," Jade thought. "Just imagine how beautiful I will look wearing all those jewels!" She set off right away.

Jade swam to a deep part of the ocean she had never been to before. She swam down and down until she found the shipwreck.

She saw the treasure chest through a porthole. Jade swam inside and reached out to touch the chest. The lid sprang open, and brilliant jewels spilled over the sides.

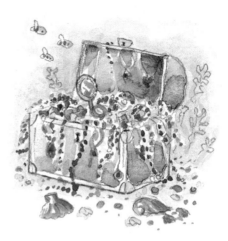

Jade lifted out a necklace and put it on. There was a little gold and silver mirror in the chest. She held it up to admire her reflection. It was beautiful! Jade looked lovelier than ever.

Suddenly, there was a loud crack, and the mirror shattered. The necklace turned to stone around her neck—it was the ship's curse! Jade tried to swim, but the necklace was so heavy, she couldn't move.

"Help!" Jade cried out. "Help! Help!"

Gentle the giant turtle had followed Jade down to the shipwreck. He heard her and swam to the porthole.

"Please help me, Gentle," cried Jade, when she saw him. Gentle's powerful flippers broke the necklace and freed Jade. As they swam away from the wreck, Gentle said, "You don't need fancy jewels, Jade. You're pretty without them."

Once she was safely home, Jade told the other mermaids that the story about the curse was true.

"And I've learned my lesson," said Jade. "I'll never be vain again."

Hazel's Comforter

Hazel loved her comforter. It was made of moss as soft as her mommy's coat, and she always kept it with her. But, one day, after she had been playing in the forest, her comforter vanished.

"Where is it?" she cried. "I can't sleep without it."

She searched the leafy forest floor. She searched the low branches of trees. It was no use—her comforter was gone.

"Borrow mine," said Squirrel. But Squirrel's comforter was too bushy.

"Borrow mine," said Hedgehog. But Hedgehog's comforter was too prickly. Hazel went to bed feeling miserable.

"Don't be sad," said her mommy. "We'll find you a new comforter tomorrow. But, tonight, snuggle up to me. I will stay with you all night long."

Hazel smiled, closed her eyes and fell fast asleep. After all, no one needs a comforter when they have a mommy to cuddle!

Rainbow Farm

Isla's fairy wand had a mind of its own. One day, while Isla was asleep, her wand came to life. POOF! Full of magical mischief, it flew out of Fairyland, looking for fun. The first thing it saw was a farm. FLASH! The pigs turned purple. WHOOSH! The trees were turquoise. SWISH! The sheep became scarlet.

"This is crazy!" neighed a pink pony.

"What's happened?" clucked a rainbow-colored hen.

Just then, Isla appeared. She had followed the trail of fairy dust. "Naughty wand, return to me!" she exclaimed. "Turn things back how they should be!"

At once, everything returned to normal. But the animals didn't look very happy.

"I loved my gold spots," wailed the rooster.

"I miss my blue tail," sniffed the cow.

"Can you change us back again?" the animals begged.

Isla laughed. And now animals come from far and wide to visit the most colorful farm in the world!

Pride Goes Before a Fall

One day, ten cloth merchants were returning to their village through the forest. Suddenly, three armed robbers jumped out in front of them and ordered the merchants to hand over all their money and possessions. Even though the merchants outnumbered the robbers, the merchants were scared, so, unhappily, they handed everything over.

The robbers were very pleased with themselves and decided to poke fun at the merchants.

"You must dance for us before we will allow you to go!" laughed one of the robbers.

Thinking they had outsmarted the poor merchants, the three robbers sat down to watch the merchants make fools of themselves.

However, there was one merchant who was very clever. Pondering their situation, he quickly hatched a plan. Then, nodding to his fellow merchants, he took the lead in the dance and started to sing a song.

"We are enty men, they are erith men. If each erith man surround eno men, eno man remains!"

Now, traders have a special language so that they can talk to each other without their buyers knowing what they are saying. The robbers didn't know this trade language—they laughed as they thought the merchants were just singing a funny song. But the other merchants knew that 'enty' means ten, 'erith' means three, and 'eno' means one. The lead merchant was saying that they were ten men, the robbers only three, and that if they pounced upon each of the robbers, nine of them could hold them down, while the remaining one could tie them up.

And this is what they did!

The robbers were completely taken by surprise. The ten merchants tied up all the robbers and took back their property. When they returned to their village, they amused their friends with the story of the silly robbers!

Bunnies All Come Out to Play

Bunnies all come out to play,
In the sunshine of the day.
They bounce and run and hop around,
Until they hear a scary sound!
At first they freeze—then off they bound,
And dart away beneath the ground.

See-saw, Margery Daw

See-saw, Margery Daw,
Johnny shall have a new master.
He shall have but a penny a day,
Because he can't work any faster.

This Little Piggy

This little piggy went to market,
This little piggy stayed at home,
This little piggy had roast beef,
This little piggy had none,
And this little piggy cried,
"Wee, wee, wee!" all the way home.

Dickery Dare

Dickery, dickery, dare,
The pig flew up in the air.
The man in brown
Soon brought him down!
Dickery, dickery, dare.

To Market, to Market

To market, to market, to buy a fat pig,
Home again, home again, jiggety-jig.
To market, to market, to buy a fat hog,
Home again, home again, jiggety-jog.
To market, to market, to buy a plum cake,
Home again, home again, market is late.
To market, to market, to buy a plum bun,
Home again, home again, market is done.

Puss in Boots

There was once an old miller who had three sons. When the miller died, he left the mill to his oldest son. The middle son was given the donkeys. The youngest son, a kind man who had always put his father and brothers before himself, was left nothing but his father's cat.

"What will become of me?" sighed the miller's young son, looking at his cat.

"Buy me a fine pair of boots, and I will help you make your fortune, just as your father had wished," replied the cat.

A talking cat! The miller's son could not believe his ears.

He bought the cat a fine pair of boots, and the two of them set off to seek their fortune.

After a while, they came to a grand palace.

"I wish I could live so grandly," sighed the miller's son.

Later, the cat went hunting and caught a rabbit. He put it in a sack and took it to the king.

"A gift from my master, the Marquis of Carabas," said the cat, pretending the miller's son was a grand nobleman.

"Now the king will want to know all about you," laughed the cat, when he told his master what he had done.

The cat delivered gifts all that week, and the king became very curious. So much so, he decided his daughter should meet this mysterious Marquis of Carabas.

The clever cat rushed back to his master, telling him to take off all his clothes and stand in the river by the side of the road.

The puzzled miller's son did as he was told, and the cat quickly hid his master's tattered clothes behind a rock.

When the cat heard the king's carriage coming, he jumped out into the road.

"Your Majesty," cried the cat, "my master's clothes were stolen while he was bathing in the river."

The king gave the miller's son a suit of fine clothes to wear and invited him into the carriage.

The miller's son looked very handsome in his new suit, and the king's daughter fell in love with him at once.

Meanwhile, the cat quickly ran on ahead. Every time he met people working in the fields, he told them, "If the king stops to ask who owns this land, you must tell him it belongs to the Marquis of Carabas."

Beyond the fields, the cat reached a grand castle belonging to a fierce ogre. The cat bravely knocked on the door and called out, "I have heard that you are a very clever ogre, and I would like to see what tricks you can do."

The ogre, who liked to show off his tricks, immediately changed himself into a snarling lion.

"Very clever," said the cat, "but a lion is large, and I think it would be more impressive to change into a tiny mouse."

At once the ogre changed into a little mouse, and the cat pounced on him and ate him up!

Then the cat went into the castle. He told all the servants that their new master was the Marquis of Carabas, and that the king was coming to visit them.

When the king arrived at the castle, the cat purred, "Your Majesty, welcome to the home of the Marquis of Carabas."

The cunning cat told his master to ask the king for his daughter's hand in marriage. And that's what he did!

The king, impressed by the nobleman's wealth, agreed, and soon the Marquis of Carabas and the princess were married.

The cat was made a lord of their court and was given the most splendid clothes, which he wore proudly with his fine boots. And they all lived happily ever after.

Unicorn Magic

Once upon a time, there were two little unicorns named Lottie and Lulu, and they lived with their mother in a cave on top of a mountain.

Unicorns are magical creatures, and their twisty horns are full of spells and enchantments. But little unicorns have to learn how to use their magic … and they don't always get it right!

One day, Lottie and Lulu's mother went to visit some friends. As soon as she had trotted out of sight, Lottie and Lulu shared a big smile.

"Let's give her a surprise," said Lottie. "Let's magically tidy up the cave."

Lottie said the first spell, and purple sparkles flew out of her twisty horn and hit a messy heap of hay in the corner. But instead of tidying it up, the spell turned the hay purple.

"Let me try," said Lulu. As she said her spell, green sparkles zipped out of her twisty horn and hit a bowl of apples. They turned into beetles and scuttled off.

"Let's do the dusting," said Lottie. She tried to make the dust vanish, but it turned into a cloud of glitter instead.

"Oh no! What a mess," gasped Lulu.

Things got worse and worse. Every spell that Lottie and Lulu tried went wrong. They made their beds with honey instead of heather. They covered the ceiling with blue cornflowers. They turned the ribbons that their mother decorated her mane with into butterflies.

And that was when their mother came back.

"Oh dear," she said, looking around at the chaos.

"We're sorry," said Lulu. "We were trying to help, but every spell went wrong."

Their mother nuzzled them both.

"It's all right," she said. "It is a bit messy, but I don't think I have ever seen the cave looking so pretty and colorful!"

Tickly, Tickly

Tickly, tickly, on your knee,
If you laugh, then you love me.

Build a House with Five Bricks

Build a house with five bricks,
One, two, three, four, five.
Put a roof on top,
And a chimney too,
Where the wind blows through!
WHOO! WHOOOO!

The Broom Song

Here's a large one for the lady,
Here's a small one for the baby;
Come buy, come buy, my lady,
Come buy o' me a broom.

The Magic Porridge Pot

Once upon a time, a poor girl named Polly lived with her mother in a small village. One day, Polly's mother became ill and could not go to work. Soon there was no money to buy food.

Polly went to the owner of a shop to ask for work. The shopkeeper reluctantly agreed to let Polly help in the shop for a cup of oats a day.

At the end of each day, Polly hurried home with her cup of oats. Then she cooked porridge for her sick mother.

The work in the shop was very tiring, and one morning, Polly knocked over a stack of bowls by mistake.

"Clumsy girl!" shouted the shopkeeper. "Leave and don't come back!"

So poor Polly went home without her cup of oats. How was she to look after her mother now? She began to weep.

Suddenly, a wizard appeared. He gave Polly a shiny cooking pot and said, "Cook, porridge, cook."

All at once, the pot was full of hot porridge.

"Remember the magic words," the wizard told Polly, giving her the pot, "and you will always have some porridge to eat."

"Oh, thank you," said Polly.

From then on, Polly and her mother were never hungry again.

The Princess and the Pea

Once upon a time, a king and queen lived in their castle with their only son. They were growing old, and it wouldn't be long before the prince would need to take up the throne. But before he became king, the prince wanted to find a princess to be his wife. He wanted her to be clever and funny and loving and kind.

The prince traveled the world in search of a real princess, but none of the princesses he met was quite right.

Then, one stormy night, there was a loud knock on the castle door.

"Who could be out on such a terrible night?" cried the queen.

The king rose to his feet. "Whoever it is, we must let them in and offer them shelter."

The prince helped his father pull open the castle's heavy doors. To their astonishment, a girl was standing outside, shivering in the rain.

"Good evening," she said politely. "Please may I come in? I was traveling when I lost my way. I'm cold and wet."

"You poor thing," cried the queen. "You must stay here."

The prince could not stop staring at the beautiful girl. "What's your name?" he asked.

"I'm Princess Sophia," she replied.

At the word "princess", the king looked at the queen. The queen smiled and took the girl's hand.

"Let's get you some dry clothes," she said.

That evening, over supper, the prince chatted with the charming girl. She was everything he had dreamed of, and by the end of the evening he had fallen in love!

The queen was happy for her son, but she wanted to make sure Sophia was a real princess.

She got her maid to help her pile up twenty mattresses on the guest bed. Under the bottom mattress she placed a tiny pea.

Then the queen showed Sophia to her room. "Sleep well, my dear," she said.

The next morning, the queen asked Sophia how she had slept. Sophia looked pale and tired.

"Not too well, I'm afraid," said the girl. "There was a hard lump in the bed, and now I'm covered with bruises."

On hearing these words, the queen laughed and hugged Sophia tightly.

"We have found our princess!" she cried. "Only a real princess would be delicate enough to feel a tiny pea through so many mattresses!"

"I knew it!" grinned the king.

The prince dropped down on one knee.

"Sophia, would you do me the honor of marrying me?" he asked.

Princess Sophia's eyes sparkled with happiness.

"Yes," she nodded. "I will!"

The prince married his bride that very day, and they all lived happily ever after.

This all happened a long time ago. If you are passing by the castle, be sure to visit its museum. There's a very special exhibit on display, in a dusty glass case—a tiny, shriveled pea! Proof of a real princess.

Sing a Song of Sixpence

Sing a song of sixpence,
A pocket full of rye.
Four and twenty blackbirds
Baked in a pie.
When the pie was opened,
The birds began to sing.
Now wasn't that a dainty dish
To set before the king?

Horsie, Horsie

Horsie, horsie, don't you stop,
Just let your feet go clippety clop,
Your tail goes swish,
And the wheels go round,
Giddy up, you're homeward bound!

The Lion and the Unicorn

The lion and the unicorn were fighting for the crown,
The lion beat the unicorn all around the town.
Some gave them white bread,
And some gave them brown,
Some gave them plum cake
And drummed them out of town.

Ride a Cock Horse

Ride a cock horse to Banbury Cross
To see a fine lady upon a white horse.
With rings on her fingers and bells on her toes,
She shall have music wherever she goes.

Mary Had a Little Lamb

Mary had a little lamb,
Its fleece was white as snow,
And everywhere that Mary went
The lamb was sure to go.
It followed her to school one day,
Which was against the rule.
It made the children laugh and play
To see a lamb at school.

I Love My Grandma

Little Hedgehog and Grandma Hedgehog loved to play hide-and-seek together. One day, when Grandma went to find Little Hedgehog to help her make a picnic, he hid behind a bush.

"Where can Little Hedgehog be?" said Grandma.

Little Hedgehog giggled.

"Oh, well. I shall just have to make the picnic myself," said Grandma.

Little Hedgehog followed closely behind Grandma.

"I wish Little Hedgehog were here to help me pick juicy blackberries," said Grandma.

When she wasn't looking, Little Hedgehog picked the biggest blackberries he could reach and put them into Grandma's basket!

"What a lot of berries!" said Grandma, surprised. "I have enough for baking now."

Little Hedgehog scampered into Grandma's kitchen to find the best place to hide. He crouched down low so that Grandma couldn't see him.

"If only Little Hedgehog were here to help me," said Grandma.

Little Hedgehog licked his lips as Grandma Hedgehog poured sweet, scrumptious honey into her mixing bowl.

When Grandma wasn't looking, Little Hedgehog crept out from his hiding place to taste the honey. Then he quickly hid again.

"Someone has been tasting my honey," said Grandma. "And they have left sticky footprints!"

Grandma followed the teeny, tiny, sticky footprints across the kitchen and out into the garden.

"Someone has been playing hide-and-seek with me!" she said.

The sticky footprints went round and round the garden and stopped by the flowerpots.

"I've found you, Little Hedgehog!" cried Grandma.

But Little Hedgehog wasn't behind the flowerpots! He was … inside one!

"Surprise!" laughed Little Hedgehog.

"Well done, Little Hedgehog," said Grandma. "You're the best at hide-and-seek. I hope you're hungry, because our picnic is ready!"

"I am hungry," said Little Hedgehog, eagerly looking around the garden. "But where is the picnic?"

Grandma giggled. "You have to find it!" she said.

Little Hedgehog searched around the garden and soon found honey cookies and fruit salad.

Then Grandma brought out a giant blackberry cake.

"Yum! I love Grandma's picnics!" Little Hedgehog shouted happily. "And … I love my grandma!"

The Greedy Pup

Mr. and Mrs. Dog were very busy animals. They had five puppies to look after! Chocolate and Coffee had brown spots, Sunny and Daffodil had yellow spots, and Custard was yellow all over.

Custard's brothers and sisters were always being called "good dog." They never barked too loudly or chewed up slippers. They never jumped on the sofa or got mud on their collars.

But Custard was always up to mischief … especially when it came to food. If there were snacks to be found, then you could be sure that Custard would find them.

One morning, the Dog family were eating their breakfast together. Chocolate and Sunny had a friendly tug-of-war, while Daffodil and Coffee gnawed on their bones. Custard, who had already finished his bone, saw that no one was looking and drank everyone else's milk. His tummy gave a loud rumble.

"Was that thunder?" asked Mr. Dog.

"Where has all the milk gone?" asked Mrs. Dog.

Custard thought that this was a good time to go for a walk. He was still hungry after breakfast, and he was very good at finding a few extra tidbits to keep him going until lunchtime.

First, he visited the hot dog stand at the end of the road. He rose up on his hind legs and panted. The man selling hot dogs grinned at him.

"All right, you bold little pup," he said. "Have a hot dog!" He flipped a hot dog into a roll and smothered it with mustard. Then he sent it spinning through the air, and Custard caught it and ate it up in three gulps.

But Custard was still hungry, so he ran down to the ice-cream stand. The ice-cream seller was busily mixing different flavors.

"Hello, Custard!" she exclaimed. "Will you help me taste some new flavors?"

Custard could hardly wait. He tried mint and raspberry, and caramel and banana, but his favorite was apple and cinnamon. He had three scoops, a cone, and a wafer.

Next, Custard visited his friend Patch's café. All the customers smiled when they saw him licking his lips. One shared her toast with him, another gave him some scrambled eggs, while a third handed him a plate of baked beans, sausages and grilled vegetables. Custard wolfed it all down.

Soon, Custard started to make his way home. He was beginning to feel a bit full.

The ginger cat on his street had a bowl of cat treats outside her house. She offered some to Custard. He tried one, but he didn't like it at all.

"Now I feel really full," he thought.

The dog on the corner had a bowl full of delicious-looking biscuits, but Custard didn't ask to share it. He padded by without even as much as a sniff.

Custard was almost home when he spotted a large cake sitting on the doorstep outside his house. It had yellow frosting with white flowers all over it. Custard looked around, but no one seemed to own it.

"It wouldn't be fair to leave this cake here on its own," he said. "Cakes are meant to be eaten. Even if I don't want it, I know my family will!"

He carefully picked up the plate in his teeth and took it inside. His mother was waiting for him.

"Custard, you naughty pup," she started to say. Then she stopped and looked at the cake he was carrying.

"You found it!" she cried. "I couldn't remember where I'd put it. We were going to surprise you with it after breakfast!"

Custard put the plate down and saw the writing on the top. "HAPPY BIRTHDAY, CUSTARD!"

"I forgot it was my birthday!" he said. "Thanks, everyone."

But Custard was still not feeling hungry. So he let his family dig into the cake.

Barking and cheering, his brothers and sisters bounded over. Soon the whole cake had disappeared. Then they snuggled up together and snoozed in the family basket.

Custard smiled in his sleep. He didn't mind about not eating his birthday cake—he knew an amazing bakery around the corner. He might visit it tomorrow!

The Perfect Pet

Emily was visiting her friend Ethan's farm to choose a puppy. Most of the puppies bounded around the barn, barking and jumping on each other. But one puppy gently pressed against Emily's legs and licked her knees.

"I like this one," said Emily, looking at the puppy's cute brown fur.

"Are you sure?" asked Ethan. "Rusty doesn't chase sticks and run around like the other puppies."

Rusty's ears drooped, and he pressed closer to Emily. It was true—he wasn't like the others. But Emily looked down at his sad eyes and smiled at him.

"Look, he's so gentle and kind," said Emily, tickling Rusty's ears. "He's the perfect pet for me!"

Rusty's heart leaped with happiness, and he wagged his little tail. And Emily knew that she had found the most perfect pet in the whole, wide world.

The Secret Cat Circus

Every morning, when they went to work, Jessie's owners left her dozing in the sunniest corner of the backyard. They thought she was a very sleepy cat, but Jessie had a secret. As soon as they had gone, Jessie pulled on a sparkly costume and went to work too … at the cat circus hidden at the end of their yard!

"Step right up!" the tabby circus-master shouted to the gathering crowd. "Come and see the best tightrope-walking cat in the whole wide world!"

The crowd gasped as Jessie walked the tightrope, balancing a fish on her nose and juggling balls of string.

By five o'clock the circus show was over and Jessie pulled off her costume, settling down to doze in the sun for when her owners came home.

"That cat could sleep all day!" Jessie's owners cried each evening.

Little did they know of her performing talent, or where the sparkles in her fur came from!

Swimming Lessons

Mommy Duck was a very busy duck indeed. "I'm going to visit my sick friend Mrs. Goose and take her some food," she told her five babies. "I want you all to be good and do lots of swimming practice while I'm gone."

"We will," said Charlotte Duck. And all her brothers and sisters nodded and promised. But as soon as Mrs. Duck had disappeared from sight, the ducklings jumped, splashed, and belly-flopped into the water. They lay on lily pads and spun around until they felt dizzy. They tipped upside down and waggled their legs in the air.

"Those aren't your lessons!" exclaimed a nearby frog. "You should follow the rules."

"Jumping and splashing is much more fun than following the rules!" replied the five little ducks.

"You're going to be in trouble," said the frog, hopping away.

The ducklings looked at each other. Now they felt sad. They hadn't meant to be naughty, and they didn't want to get into trouble, so they sat quietly on the bank of the stream.

Just then, they heard Mommy Duck singing as she swam home. Bravely, they told her what had happened. Mommy Duck listened carefully. Then she smiled.

"Well, even though you didn't follow your swimming lessons properly," said Mommy Duck, wrapping her soft wings around them, "I'm pleased that you told me the truth. Now, let's practice swimming together."

After swimming practice, Mommy Duck told her ducklings that the lesson was over and it was time to play. Then with a big SPLASH, she belly-flopped into the stream!

"After all, you learn best when you're having fun!" she said.

The Butterfly Ballerina

Isabella Ballerina loved ballet. Best of all, she liked going to Madame Colette's Ballet School.

"Let us practice our ballet positions!" called Madame Colette one morning, clapping her hands. "No, no, Isabella! You are pointing the wrong foot again!"

"Sorry!" Isabella said. "I'm always getting my left and right mixed up!"

"Now, girls," cried Madame Colette. "I have exciting news to announce! We will be putting on our first show, the Butterfly Ballet. I will choose girls to play raindrop butterflies and rainbow butterflies, and one girl to dance as the sunshine butterfly!"

Back home, Isabella told Mom all about the ballet show.

"I just wish I could remember my left from my right!" she sighed.

Mom smiled. "This might help." She gave Isabella a beautiful butterfly bracelet. "Wear it on your right wrist. Then you'll always be able to tell which way is right."

At each ballet lesson, Isabella kept looking at her butterfly bracelet to make sure she turned the right way!

Finally, after many rehearsals, Madame Colette told the girls their roles.

"Isabella, you shall play the sunshine butterfly. As you twirl so beautifully, you will dance the final pirouette!" said Madame Colette.

Isabella smiled. She just hoped she would turn the right way!

The week before the show, Isabella practiced her pirouettes everywhere! She twirled in the backyard … in her bedroom … and at the park.

On the night of the big show, all the girls dressed in tutus and shimmering butterfly wings. The lights dimmed. Beautiful music filled the room. The ballet was about to begin!

The raindrop and rainbow butterflies danced gracefully from flower to flower.

At last it was Isabella's turn to dance. Nervously, she touched her butterfly bracelet. Then, taking a deep breath, she twirled the most perfect pirouette she had ever twirled!

The girls joined Isabella on stage, and they all curtsied.

"Oops!" giggled Isabella. She had curtsied with the wrong foot forward, but it didn't matter one little bit.

She would always be Isabella, Butterfly Ballerina!

A, B, C

A, B, C,
Our kitty's up the tree!
And now begins,
With a sneeze and a cough
To lick her long white stockings off.
No more she'll go into the snow.
Not she, not she, not she!

Little Wind

Little wind, blow on the hilltop;
Little wind, blow down the plain;
Little wind, blow up the sunshine,
Little wind, blow off the rain.

Twitching Whiskers

Twitching whiskers,
Big long ears,
Little bobtails
On their rears,
Still as statues,
One, two, three—
Then hippety hoppety,
You can't catch me!

The Wise Old Owl

There was an old owl who lived in an oak;
The more he heard, the less he spoke.
The less he spoke, the more he heard.
Why aren't we like that wise old bird?

In April

In April's sweet month,
When leaves start to spring,
Lambs skip like fairies,
And birds build and sing.

There Was an Old Crow

There was an old crow
Sat upon a clod:
There's an end of my song,
That's odd!

The Peacock's Complaint

Peacock was very unhappy about his ugly voice, and he spent most of his days complaining about it to anyone who would listen.

One day, Fox had had enough of Peacock's constant moaning.

"It is true that you cannot sing," he said, "but look how beautiful you are. Your feathers are amazing!"

Peacock looked at his feathers.

"Oh, what good is all this beauty," he groaned, "if I have such an unpleasant voice?"

Fox sighed. "Everyone has their own special gift. You have your beauty, the nightingale has his song, the owl has his eyes, and the eagle has his strength."

But Peacock continued to moan.

"Even if you had a musical voice," Fox shouted in frustration, "you would find something else to complain about!"

And the moral of this story is: Do not envy the gifts of others. Make the most of your own.

The Goose That Laid the Golden Eggs

A farmer and his wife owned a very special goose. Every day, the goose would lay a golden egg. The couple sold the eggs, and before long, they became rich.

The goose continued to lay her golden eggs, and the farmer and his wife got richer and richer. But, sadly, they also became greedy. In spite of their great wealth, they were not satisfied.

One day, the farmer's wife turned to her husband and said, "Just think, if we could have all the golden eggs that are in this goose, we could be even richer, even more quickly!"

The farmer grinned at his wife.

"You're right," he cried. "We wouldn't have to wait for her to lay an egg every day."

So, the greedy couple killed the goose. Of course, she was like every other goose. She had no golden eggs inside her at all. And that was the end of the golden eggs!

And the moral of this story is: Too much greed results in nothing.

Pig's Bath Time

Pig enjoyed being muddy. He loved rolling in ditches, digging in flowerbeds, and jumping in muddy puddles. The farmer usually didn't mind Pig being mucky. But the day before the county fair, the farmer said something that made Pig tremble: "It's time for Pig to have a bath!"

When Pig heard the word "bath," he started to run. The farmer chased him all around the grubby pigsty, across the boggy meadow, through the grimy cattle barn, and straight into the stinky sheep pen.

"Now you definitely need a bath," said the farmer in a firm voice. "And so do I!"

But Pig struggled in the farmer's arms, and the farmer couldn't get a hand free to run the bath. So the farmer's wife and son came to help.

First they lifted Pig into the bathtub. Then they turned on the faucets. SPLISH! SPLASH! Pig squealed and kicked his legs, and everyone got very wet.

The farmer's wife picked up a bottle of pig shampoo and squirted some into her hands. Then she rubbed it all over Pig's head. Pig let out a loud "OINK!" and then sniffed it. Suddenly, Pig realized he smelled good!

The farmer, his wife, and their son scrubbed, rubbed, and polished until Pig was as clean as a whistle. Pig felt wonderfully warm and clean.

Then the farmer's son dried Pig with a fluffy blanket.

"He'll be the cleanest pig at the farm show," said the boy.

Pig gave a happy smile. He had quite enjoyed his bath. From now on, he decided, he would have a bath every day!

Sick Little Bunny

Bunny did not feel well. Her little twitchy nose felt all snuffly.

"ATCHOO!" she sneezed loudly.

"Oh, my poor little bunny," said her mommy. "I think you've caught a cold."

So Mommy gently tucked Bunny into her bed.

"You need to rest and stay warm," she told her.

"But I don't want to!" sniffled Bunny. "I want to go outside and play!"

Mommy wiped Bunny's sneezy nose and kissed her softly on her fluffy ears.

"Snuggle under your covers and go to sleep now. I'll come and check on you in a little while," she said, as she quietly closed the bedroom door.

But as soon as Mommy had gone, Bunny got out of bed. Her legs felt wobbly and her body ached.

"Come on, Teddy, let's go!" she told her cuddly toy. "We're going outside!"

Shaking and shivering, Bunny slowly crawled downstairs. She was just reaching for the front door handle when Mommy suddenly appeared behind her.

"Bunny!" Mommy scolded. "Where are you going?"

Then Mommy scooped Bunny up into her warm arms and carried her into the den.

"Let's snuggle up on the sofa, and I'll read you a story," she said softly. "Then, if you feel a little better, you can go outside."

Bunny smiled and hugged her mommy tightly.

"Thank you," she sighed.

But as Mommy started to read Bunny's favorite book, Bunny's eyes began to feel heavy, and her ears flopped forward.

It was warm and cozy next to Mommy and before long, Bunny was fast asleep.

"Sweet dreams, my little one," Mommy whispered, and she gently carried Bunny back to her bed.

Flying High, Swooping Low

Flying high, swooping low,
Loop-the-loop and round they go.
Catching currents, soaring fast,
Feathered friends come sweeping past.

Birds of a Feather

Birds of a feather flock together,
And so will pigs and swine;
Rats and mice shall have their choice,
And so shall I have mine.

The Rooster Crows

The rooster's on the wood pile
Blowing his horn,
The bull's in the barn
A-threshing the corn.

Brown Owl

The brown owl sits in the ivy bush,
And she looketh wondrous wise,
With a horny beak beneath her cowl,
And a pair of large round eyes.

Little Friend

In the greenhouse lives a wren,
Little friend of little men;
When they're good she tells them where
To find the apple, quince and pear.

Cock Robin's Courtship

Cock Robin got up early
At the break of day,
And went to Jenny's window
To sing a roundelay.
He sang Cock Robin's love
To little Jenny Wren,
And when he got unto the end
Then he began again.

127

Pinkabella and the Fairy Goldmother

Pinkabella loved pink *almost* more than anything else …
and she loved LOTS of things, like playing with her friend,
Violet, and spending time with her godmother, Auntie Alura.

Pinkabella often thought her auntie might be a fairy
godmother. She always looked so sparkly and magical!

One day, while Pinkabella and Violet were playing in
Pinkabella's bedroom, Auntie Alura came to visit.

"Auntie," cried Pinkabella, flying into her godmother's arms.

"It's lovely to see you too, Pinkabella," Auntie Alura laughed,
hugging her back. "Is this your room? It's very …"

"PINKTASTIC!" beamed Pinkabella.

"PINKERRIFIC!" added Violet.

"Er, yes," said Auntie Alura, casting her eye around Pinkabella's things. "Although I've always preferred gold, myself!"

Pinkabella looked at her auntie's gold dress, gold shoes, and gold bag, and grinned. Auntie Alura really *did* like gold!

"Maybe she's my fairy GOLDmother," Pinkabella whispered to Violet with a giggle.

Just then, Pinkabella's dad called up from the backyard. "Pinkabella! Violet! Come and get a drink." And the two friends rushed downstairs, leaving Auntie Alura alone in the bedroom.

A while later, after Auntie Alura had joined them outside, Pinkabella and Violet returned upstairs.

"Eek!" gasped Pinkabella as she opened her bedroom door. "My pinktacular room is all… GOLD!"

"B-but how?" asked Violet, in shock.

Suddenly, Pinkabella saw a sparkly stick on her bed.
"This looks like a wand," she gasped.
"Do you think it's magic?" asked Violet.
Pinkabella grabbed the stick. "Let's try it!"
She waved the wand and said, "Make everything
PINKTASTIC again!"
The wand made a fizzing noise, and pink
sparkles shot out of the end....

130

The sparkles whizzed through the air, and everything they landed on turned bright pink.

"Wow! It IS real," cried Violet. "Let me try it!"

Pinkabella threw the wand to Violet, but it bounced off the wall and flew out of the open window.

Pinkabella and Violet watched in horror as the wand twirled away, shooting pink sparkles down into the yard.

Pinkabella and Violet ran outside. Everything had turned pink, including Pinkabella's mom, dad, and auntie!

"My wand!" cried Auntie Alura. "What's it doing out here?"

"I found it on my bed," replied Pinkabella. "I'm really sorry, Auntie Alura. I didn't know it was your wand. I just wanted my room to be pink again."

"It's okay. I'm sorry, too," said her auntie. "I wanted to see what your room would look like in gold, but then I forgot to change it to pink again. I must have left my wand behind by mistake."

After Auntie Alura had turned everything back to normal, Pinkabella asked her why she had a wand.

"I'm your fairy godmother, of course," she whispered. Pinkabella gasped in delight. She had been right all along!

Then Auntie Alura added a touch of gold to Pinkabella's dress.

"Pink and gold together," laughed Pinkabella. "It's magical!"

Surf Frog

Francisca the frog always won the gold medal at the Sandy Beach Surf Contest.

"None of you can beat me," she told the other surfers on the seafront. But, just then, a young frog whizzed toward her on a skateboard. CRASH! The skateboard hurt Francisca's leg.

"Oh no!" cried Francisca. "I won't be able to surf with a sore leg!"

Poor Francisca limped home and shut the door. Her friend Lottie followed her.

"Come back to Sandy Beach to watch the competition with me," Lottie said.

"No, thanks," said Francisca. "If I can't win, I don't want to be there. Winning is all that matters."

But Lottie didn't agree.

"There are lots of young frogs hopping around on the beach with nothing to do," she said. "You could help them."

So, on the first day of the competition, Francisca arrived at Sandy Beach feeling very grumpy. She showed the young frogs how to stand up on a surfboard. They all had a good time, and suddenly Francisca found herself smiling.

Next day, she showed them how to paddle their surfboards in the water.

"You're a great teacher!" said one of the young frogs. Francisca felt proud.

Francisca worked hard to help the young frogs learn to surf.

On the last day of the competition, they put on a surfing show for the crowd. Everyone cheered and clapped, and Francisca was so excited that she forgot all about the competition. The young frogs mattered more than any medal.

"Are you okay?" Lottie asked her, when the medals were handed out.

"I feel great," said Francisca, smiling. "Now I remember how much fun it is just to surf. It's not winning I love. It's surfing!"

Hickety Pickety

Hickety Pickety, my black hen,
She lays eggs for gentlemen,
Sometimes nine, and sometimes ten,
Hickety Pickety, my black hen.

Cluck, Cluck, Cluck

Cluck, cluck, cluck, cluck, cluck,
Good morning, Mrs. Hen.
How many chickens have you got?
Madam, I've got ten.
Four of them are yellow,
And four of them are brown.
And two of them are speckled red,
The nicest in the town.

I Had a Little Hen

I had a little hen, the prettiest ever seen,
She washed up the dishes, and kept the house clean.
She went to the mill to fetch me some flour,
And always got home in less than an hour.
She baked me my bread, she brewed me my ale,
She sat by the fire and told a fine tale!

Can You Walk on Tiptoe?

Can you walk on tiptoe, as softly as a cat?
And can you slink along the road, softly, just like that?
Can you take enormous strides, like a great giraffe?
Or wibble-wobble-wibble just like a new-born calf?

There Was a Crooked Man

There was a crooked man
And he walked a crooked mile,
He found a crooked sixpence
Upon a crooked stile.
He bought a crooked cat,
Which caught a crooked mouse,
And they all lived together
In a little crooked house.

Magical Shoes

Lily the ballerina was hurrying to the theater. Today was the day of the grand ballet. Lily was dancing with her friends Wanda, Amber, and Tilly. They were all looking forward to dancing with Fleur.

Fleur was the Prima Ballerina. She always danced in a magical pair of silver ballet shoes. Only the Prima Ballerina could wear them. They would not work if anyone else wore them.

The four friends watched Fleur during the first dance as she performed a perfect plié, a beautiful arabesque, and a stunning pirouette. They all loved dancing with Fleur.

After the first dance, everyone hurried to change their costumes for the next dance. Suddenly, Fleur appeared in her bare feet, looking upset.

"Something terrible has happened!" Fleur exclaimed. "I took off my silver ballet shoes for a moment, and now they have gone. I won't be able to dance until they are found."

"Don't worry," said Lily kindly. "We'll find them for you."

"We'll find the shoes in time for the next dance,"
Wanda promised.

The four friends ran outside. As Lily wondered which way
she should go, she spotted a magpie flying toward the woods.
She could see something silver in its beak.

"The silver shoes!" gasped Lily.
"The magpie must have stolen them!"

Lily ran after the magpie as fast as she
could. But meanwhile, the ballet shoes
grew too heavy for the magpie. They
fell from its beak.

The shoes dropped right in front of
Wanda, who was searching the woods.

"The magical shoes!" she said.
"How beautiful they are. I'll just try them
on quickly."

But as soon as Wanda put on the magical shoes, a strange
thing happened. She suddenly danced a plié. She pliéd up and
down and up and down, until she realized she couldn't stop.

Wanda pliéd out of the woods and into the meadow.
Soon her legs were so tired she couldn't dance anymore.

She fell flat on her back
into a nearby bush.

"Are you all right?"
asked Amber, who
had been searching
the meadow.

"Yes, thanks," puffed Wanda. "But help me take the shoes off."
Amber pulled off the magical shoes and gazed at them.

"They're so beautiful," she said. "I'm sure no one would
mind if I tried them on quickly."

Amber tried on the magical
shoes and danced a
perfect arabesque.

"I never knew I could
arabesque so well!" she thought.

Then she did another, and
another, until she realized that she couldn't stop.

"Help! I can't stop!" poor Amber called as she danced out
of the meadow and into the garden. She was so dizzy from
dancing that she ended up in the fountain with a big splash.

Luckily, Tilly was nearby and ran to help. But when she saw
the silver shoes lying on the ground, she just couldn't resist
putting them on.

"They're so beautiful," she said. "I'm sure no one would
mind if I tried them on quickly."

But when Tilly tried on the magical shoes a strange
thing happened. She started to pirouette around
and around....

"Wheee ... this is fun!"
exclaimed Tilly. "I never
knew I could
pirouette
so well!"

But then she began to spin faster and faster, and realized that she couldn't stop.

Poor Tilly pirouetted down the hill, straight into a muddy puddle.

The others caught up with her and helped her up.

Lily carefully took the precious ballet shoes off Tilly's feet.

"They are so beautiful," said Lily, and she wanted to try them on too. But, in her heart, she knew that there was only one person who was meant to wear them.

"Let's return the shoes to the Prima Ballerina," Lily said to the others. "She'll be so happy we found them."

"My shoes!" exclaimed Fleur when Lily and the others returned. "Thank you! Now we must get on with the show!"

But Wanda, Amber, and Tilly were in such a mess they couldn't go back on stage.

"Oh dear!" Fleur sighed. "You won't be able to dance looking like that." Then Fleur turned to Lily with a smile. "We will have to dance together."

Lily danced alone with the Prima Ballerina. And they danced so beautifully together that everyone clapped and cheered more than ever.

"I'll remember this evening for ever and ever," thought Lily, as she walked to the front of the stage and took her final bow.

Why the Sun and the Moon Live in the Sky

Long ago, the Sun and the Water were great friends, and they both lived on the Earth together. The Sun visited the Water often, but the Water never returned his visits.

At last the Sun asked his friend why he never visited. The Water replied that the Sun's house was not big enough, and that if he came with all his family, he would drive the Sun out of his home.

"If you want me to visit you," the Water added, "you will have to build a very large house. I have a huge family, and we take up a lot of room."

The Sun promised to build a very large house, and soon afterwards, he returned home to his wife, the Moon.

The Sun told the Moon what he had promised the Water, and the next day, they began building a large house to entertain the Water and all his family.

After several weeks, the house was complete and the Sun asked the Water to come and visit him.

When the Water arrived, he called out to the Sun and asked whether it would be safe to enter.

"Yes, of course. Come in," replied the Sun.

The Water began to flow in, followed by the fish and all the other animals and creatures that belonged to the Water.

Very soon, the Water was knee-deep in the house.

"Is it still safe for us to come in?" called out the Water.

"Yes, of course," replied the Sun. So more of the Water's family came in.

When the Water was at the level of a man's head, the Water said to the Sun, "Do you want more of my family to come?"

Not knowing any better, the Sun and the Moon both said that everyone was welcome. More and more of the Water's family came in, until the Sun and the Moon had to sit on top of their roof.

Every so often, the Water asked the Sun if it was still okay to come in. Each time, the Sun and the Moon answered yes.

Soon, the Water overflowed the top of the roof, and the Sun and the Moon couldn't see their house anymore.

As the Water rose higher and higher, the Sun and the Moon climbed up into the sky…. And they've been there ever since!

Pixie Pool

Lilian wasn't enjoying her day at the beach.
"I'll never learn to swim," she said. Even with floats and water wings, Lilian found swimming difficult. So she went to explore some rock pools. One of them sparkled like diamonds. When Lilian peered more closely, she saw a pixie sitting beside the pool. Lilian gasped in surprise.

"Please don't tell anyone you saw me!" cried the pixie. "If you keep my secret, I'll grant you a wish. What will it be?"

"Please can you make me swim as gracefully as a dolphin?" Lilian asked.

The pixie smiled. Just then, Lilian heard dolphin voices calling to her from the sea. "We'll help you!" they said.

Lilian splashed into the water, and the dolphins jumped and dove around her.

"This is fun!" Lilian said, joining in. Suddenly, she was gliding through the water, just like the dolphins.

When they left, Lilian waved and kept on splashing. She couldn't wait for her next beach trip!

Show Time!

Isabelle the rabbit and her friends looked forward to the woodland summer show all year long. But this year, there was a problem.

"The show's canceled!" cried Hazel the mouse. "This year's act, The Amazing Moles, are all sick in bed."

The other animals felt gloomy—except Isabelle.

"We're not giving up that easily," she said. "We can put on the show."

"How?" asked Marcus the squirrel.

"Practice makes perfect," said Isabelle.

So the friends rehearsed their favorite dance routines, jokes, and magic tricks, while the audience gathered. Then the show began with a tap dance by Hazel and her sister Jessica. Marcus told jokes, and Gabriel the owl did magic. Finally, Isabelle performed a ballet dance. The crowd went wild!

"Being in the show was even more fun than watching it," said Isabelle, hugging her friends. "Let's do it again next year!"

Minnie and Winnie

Minnie and Winnie
Slept in a shell.
Sleep, little ladies!
And they slept well.

Pink was the shell within,
Silver without;
Sounds of the great sea
Wandered about.

Sleep, little ladies,
Wake not soon!
Echo on echo
Dies to the moon.

Two bright stars
Peeped into the shell.
"What are they dreaming of?
Who can tell?"

Started a green linnet
Out of the croft;
Wake, little ladies,
The sun is aloft!

Little Jumping Joan

Here am I, little jumping Joan.
When nobody's with me,
I'm always alone.

Lady Moon

Lady Moon, Lady Moon,
Where are you roving?
Over the sea.
Lady Moon, Lady Moon,
Whom are you loving?
All that love me.
Are you not tired with
Rolling, and never
Resting to sleep?
Why look so pale,
And so sad, as if for ever
Wishing to weep?

The Snow Queen

Once, there was a wicked demon who made a magic mirror. Everything it reflected looked ugly and mean. One day, the mirror smashed into tiny specks, and the specks got into people's eyes and made everything look bad to them. Some specks became caught in people's hearts, making them feel grumpy.

A few of the specks from the mirror floated toward a faraway place where there lived two best friends, a girl named Gerda and a boy named Kay.

The pair spent endless days together. In the winter, Gerda's grandmother told them wonderful stories while the snow swirled outside.

"The Snow Queen brings the winter weather," she would say. "She peeps in at the windows and leaves icy patterns on the glass."

In the summer, the children would play in the little roof garden between their houses.

One sunny day, they were reading together when Kay let out a cry. Specks from the demon's magic mirror had caught in Kay's eye and his heart.

Kay became bad-tempered throughout summer and fall, and was still cross when winter came.

One snowy day, he stormed off with his sled. Suddenly, a large white sleigh swept past, and Kay mischievously hitched his sled to the back.

The sleigh pulled him far, far away. When it finally stopped, Kay realized the sleigh belonged to the Snow Queen from Gerda's grandmother's story! The Snow Queen kissed Kay's forehead, and her icy touch froze his heart. He forgot all about Gerda and his home.

Back home, Gerda missed Kay. She searched everywhere for him. Just as she was about to give up, Gerda noticed a little boat among the rushes down by the river.

"Perhaps the river will carry me to Kay," she thought. She climbed in, and the boat glided away.

Many hours later, the boat reached the shore. A large raven came hopping toward Gerda.

"I have seen your friend," the raven croaked. "A young man who sounds like him has married a princess. I'll take you there."

That night, the raven took Gerda to the palace. But the prince wasn't Kay.

Poor Gerda! She was far from home. She told the prince and princess her story. They promised to help her, and the next morning Gerda was given warm clothes and a golden sleigh.

She set off into the woods, but before long she was spotted by a band of robbers.

"That sleigh is pure gold!" they hissed.

The robbers sprang out and captured Gerda. Then the daughter of the robber chief appeared. The girl was lonely and excited by the thought of a new friend.

"Please, treat her gently!" the robber girl pleaded. "She can stay with me."

Gerda was grateful to the robber girl for her kindness.

Inside the robber's den, Gerda met the robber girl's pet reindeer. When Gerda told her new friend about Kay, the reindeer spoke, saying he had seen Kay with the Snow Queen.

"I know the way to the Snow Queen's palace," added the reindeer. "I will take you there."

It was a long, cold journey, but at last Gerda and the reindeer arrived outside the Snow Queen's palace.

Inside the ice palace, the Snow Queen still held Kay under her spell.

"Spring is coming," she announced suddenly. "I must leave. It is time for me to make it snow on the other side of the world!" And she flew off in her sleigh, leaving Kay alone.

At that moment, Gerda crept into the palace. When she saw her friend, she wept. Her tears fell onto his chest. They melted his cold heart. Kay began to cry too, and his tears washed the speck of glass from his eye. At last he was free of the spell!

The reindeer carried Gerda and Kay back home.

"Grandmother!" called Gerda. "We're back at last!"

The old lady hugged them tightly. She was so happy to see them.

"I knew that you would come home one day," she cried. "Now, tell me all about your adventures!"

The Princess and the Salt

Once, a rich and powerful king summoned his three daughters to his throne room on his birthday. His first daughter gave him gold, and the second daughter brought him silver. The king was very pleased with these gifts.

"I have brought you salt," said the third daughter.

"Salt!" cried the king. "How dare you insult me? What good is salt?" And he banished his own daughter from his kingdom.

But when the princess left, all the salt in the kingdom vanished. At first, the king complained that his food was tasteless, but then he became very ill from lack of salt.

The king realized how foolish he had been and sent for his daughter. When she returned to the kingdom, the salt also returned.

"Forgive me," said the king. "Your gift of salt was more precious than silver or gold, for you cannot live without salt."

From that day on, the king learned to value things other than his riches.

An Egg

In marble halls as white as milk,
Lined with skin as soft as silk;
Within a fountain crystal-clear,
A golden apple doth appear.
No doors there are to this stronghold—
Yet thieves break in and steal the gold.

A Candle

Little Nancy Etticoat
In a white petticoat,
And a red rose.
The longer she stands
The shorter she grows.

The Wind

When the wind is in the East,
'Tis neither good to man nor beast.
When the wind is in the North,
The skillful fisher goes not forth.
When the wind is in the South,
It blows the bait in the fish's mouth.
When the wind is in the West,
Then it is at its very best.

Thumbelina

Once upon a time, there was a poor woman who lived all
alone. She dreamed of having a child of her own with
whom she could share her home. One day, she decided to
visit a kindly witch who lived at the end of her lane to ask for
help.

"Take this grain and plant it in a pot," said the witch.
"Water it and care for it. The grain will do the rest."

Every morning the woman checked on her precious plant.
Within a week, it had grown into a tall flower.

"I've never seen anything so beautiful," said the woman,
bending down to give the bud a gentle kiss.

POP! The pink flower suddenly opened up its petals. Sitting
inside it was a tiny girl, no bigger than the woman's thumb.
The woman was overjoyed.

"I shall call you Thumbelina," she cried.

Thumbelina and her mother were very happy. Then, one night, while they slept, a warty toad took Thumbelina away.

"You will make the perfect wife for my son," hissed the toad, placing Thumbelina on a lily pad in the middle of a stream. Then the toad swam off to find her son.

Poor Thumbelina started to cry—she didn't want to marry a toad.

"Don't cry, little girl," said a passing fish. "I'll help you."

The kind fish nibbled through the stem of the lily pad, and it floated free downstream. At last, it drifted to the riverbank, and Thumbelina jumped off.

All summer, Thumbelina lived happily among the flowers. But when winter arrived, she was cold and hungry.

A kind field mouse invited her to spend the winter in his cozy underground burrow. It was warm and snug, but Thumbelina missed the sunlight.

One day, the mouse's friend, a mole, asked Thumbelina to marry him. Thumbelina didn't want to marry the mole and live underground. But, as the mouse had been so kind to her, Thumbelina agreed to a wedding the following summer.

As the wedding day grew closer, Thumbelina became more sad. One morning, she was miserably wandering through the underground tunnels of the mouse's home, when she came across a swallow. He was almost dead with cold.

"I will help you," said Thumbelina, hugging the bird to her.

"Thank you," sighed the swallow, "you have saved my life. I will take you to a place where the sun always shines."

Tears ran down Thumbelina's cheeks. "I can't leave," she cried. "I have to marry Mole."

"I will never forget what you have done for me," said the swallow, and he left.

Summer came around again, and the day of Thumbelina's marriage to Mole. As Thumbelina stepped outside to say goodbye to the sunshine forever, the swallow swooped down.

"Quick, come with me!" he chirped. And this time Thumbelina didn't refuse.

The land of sunshine was full of beautiful flowers. As Thumbelina reached out to touch a pretty bud, its petals opened to reveal a tiny fairy prince.

All around her, little fairies appeared.

"Will you marry me?" asked the tiny prince.

"I will!" replied Thumbelina, grinning joyfully. She knew she had found the place where she truly belonged.

Sophie's Smile

All the other fish were afraid of Sophie.
"She's always frowning," they said. "Why does she look so grumpy?" But poor Sophie wasn't really cross. That was just the shape of her mouth. She couldn't seem to smile and look friendly.

One day, Sophie had an idea.

"I'll throw a party," she said. "I'll show them that they don't have to be scared of me." She spent a long time getting everything ready. She sent out her invitations on tiny shells, and decorated a cave with coral in every color she could find. She arranged for the most famous underwater band in the sea to be there, and she lit the cave with tiny crystal jellyfish.

The guests arrived and swam shyly into the cave. They looked nervous when they said hello, and Sophie's heart sank. If only they could see that she was kind and happy! But she nodded to the band, and they began to play.

"Come and dance!" she called.

One by one, the other fish started to dance. Sophie stayed back because she didn't want to frighten anyone. But as the dancers swirled faster and faster, they saw that Sophie wasn't scary at all. She was nervous, just like them!

The whirlpool of dancing fish spun Sophie, sending her topsy-turvy. She twirled around so fast that everything about her got turned upside down … including her frown!

When the music stopped playing, and everyone stopped dancing, the other fish gathered around Sophie. They were all smiling now that they knew that Sophie was so friendly. And when they looked at her, they saw that something about her had changed too. Now she was wearing a big, happy smile!

The Sick Day

Rabbit felt sick, so his mother wrapped him up in a fluffy blanket and called Dr. Hare.

"Maybe he's got a fever," said Dr. Hare. "Cool him down with carrot salad."

Rabbit's mother made some carrot salad, but Rabbit wasn't hungry.

"Maybe he's got a cold," said Dr. Hare. "Warm him up with carrot soup."

Rabbit's mother cooked up a delicious soup, but Rabbit couldn't even eat a spoonful.

"What do you want, Rabbit?" asked Dr. Hare kindly. Rabbit pointed at his mother, who stroked his soft fur and kissed his pink nose. She gave him a big rabbity cuddle.

"I'm feeling better already," said Rabbit happily.

His mother made him giggle with some funny stories. By bedtime, Rabbit felt well again. His father came home, and Rabbit told him all about the doctor.

"I didn't need salad or soup," he said. "I needed cuddles and funny stories!"

"They're the best medicine of all," said his father wisely.

Oak Tree Hospital

One day, Mrs. Mouse arrived at Oak Tree Hospital in a fluster.

"Please help!" she cried. "My son Lucas has a thimble stuck on his head!"

The squirrel nurse tried to pull the thimble off, but Lucas yelled, "Stop!" so she did. The squirrel doctor smeared Lucas's head with honey. It made him very sticky and got in his eyes and ears, but it didn't move the thimble one bit. Then the squirrel nurse had a thought.

"Lucas, can you waggle your ears and wiggle your eyebrows?" she asked.

Lucas waggled and wiggled as hard as he could, while the squirrel nurse and Mrs. Mouse and the squirrel doctor tugged on the thimble. And with a loud POP! the thimble flew into the air and hit the squirrel doctor on the nose.

From then on, just in case, Mrs. Mouse made Lucas practice waggling and wiggling every single day, and kept him well away from thimbles!

Max and Tallulah

Max loved Tallulah with all his heart. But he was too shy to tell her. If only there was a way to make her notice him.

So Max decided to give Tallulah a present. He picked her favorite fruit, balanced it on a lily leaf, and pushed it carefully along the river.

But just before Max reached Tallulah, the leaf started to sink! All the fruit fell into the water and floated away.

Max needed another plan.

That night, by the light of the moon, Max practiced a daring dance.

When the sun began to rise, he went
to find Tallulah.

Tallulah was in the forest looking
for juicy leaves. Max was certain his
daring dance would get her attention.

He stepped forward, tapped his hoof,
and leaped into the sky. Then he twirled,
faster and faster!

Surely Tallulah would notice him now?

But Tallulah was so busy eating that she
didn't see Max or any of his daring dance.

Max needed a new idea.

He gathered leaves and flowers and insects of every size and color. Max was going to make the most magnificent hat Tallulah had ever seen!

Surely that would impress her?

But when Max appeared in his magnificent hat … Tallulah was so startled that she ran away!

Max had not meant to frighten Tallulah. What could he do now?

Suddenly, Max saw his reflection in the water and he had the greatest idea of all!

He was going to be …

… himself!

Max smiled at Tallulah, and Tallulah smiled back.
Then together they walked side by side.

Max told Tallulah all about fruit on lily leaves, a daring
dance, his magnificent hat … and being just Max!

Jack and Jill

Jack and Jill went up the hill
To fetch a pail of water;
Jack fell down and broke his crown,
And Jill came tumbling after.
Up Jack got, and home did trot
As fast as he could caper;
He went to bed to mend his head
With vinegar and brown paper.

Rain, Rain, Go Away

Rain, rain, go away,
Come again another day.
Rain, rain, go away,
Little Johnny wants to play.

Doctor Foster

Doctor Foster
Went to Gloucester
In a shower of rain.
He stepped in a puddle,
Right up to his middle,
And never went there again!

It's Raining, It's Pouring

It's raining, it's pouring,
The old man is snoring.
He went to bed and bumped his head,
And couldn't get up in the morning.

I Hear Thunder

I hear thunder, I hear thunder.
Hark, don't you? Hark, don't you?
Pitter, patter, raindrops,
Pitter, patter, raindrops.
I'm wet through! So are you!

Bobby Shaftoe's Gone to Sea

Bobby Shaftoe's gone to sea,
Silver buckles at his knee;
He'll come back and marry me,
Bonny Bobby Shaftoe!

Saskia's Fairy Ball

Saskia the fairy was organizing the fairy ball. But, on the morning of the ball, she lost her wand!

"How am I going to get everything ready for tonight without magic?" she cried.

Suddenly, she had an idea. She was good friends with the woodland animals, and she had been planning to invite them all. Perhaps they would help her!

First, Saskia had to find a place to hold the ball. Without her wand, she couldn't build a palace, so she chose a little clearing in the forest. Next, she visited the squirrels and rabbits, and explained her problem.

"Will you help me?" she asked. "I need food, decorations and music."

"We can make nut muffins," the squirrels squeaked.

"Carrot cupcakes!" the rabbits cried, hopping around.

Saskia flew up to the treetops to visit her magpie friends.

"You love sparkly things," she said. "Will you find decorations for the trees?"

The magpies agreed and flew off. Finally, Saskia asked the fireflies to light up the ball and the songbirds to provide the music.

At last, the sun went down and the stars began to twinkle. Fireflies danced above the clearing, lighting up the sparkling jewelry in the trees. Toadstool tables were piled high with cupcakes and muffins.

"It's perfect," said Saskia, dancing around with her animal friends. "Thank you so much for helping!"

The fairy guests arrived, expecting a castle and a ballroom, but when they saw the clearing, they clapped their hands in delight. The Fairy Queen stepped forward and took Saskia by the hand.

"You have done magnificently," she said. "You've made our animal friends part of the evening and created a beautiful setting for the ball. From now on, every ball shall be outside!"

Why the Hippopotamus Lives in the Water

A long time ago, there was a huge hippo. Nobody except the hippo's family knew his name.

One day, the hippo asked the other animals to guess his name. But, as the hippo had suspected, no one could get it right.

"What would you do if I told you your name?" asked a little tortoise.

"I would be so ashamed that my family and I would leave the land to live in the water," replied the hippo. "We would only come out at night to feed."

Soon, after noticing that the hippo and his family washed and drank in the lake every day, the tortoise hid by a bush and waited until they were returning home.

As the hippo's wife trailed behind her family, the tortoise crept onto the path in front of her, then ducked into his shell.

"Ouch!" cried the hippo's wife, as she bumped into the tortoise's hard shell. "Isantim, my husband, I've hurt my foot!"

Later, the tortoise told the hippo his name, and Isantim kept his promise. And that's why hippopotamuses live in the water.

How the Rabbit Lost His Tail

Mrs. Cat was very jealous of Mr. Rabbit's long tail, as she didn't have one. So Mrs. Cat stole Mr. Rabbit's fine tail. Then she took a needle and thread out of her basket and sewed the tail onto her own body.

"It looks so much better on me!" Mrs. Cat purred happily.

"I found my tail too long, anyway," Mr. Rabbit replied. "You can keep it if you give me your basket." So she did.

And Mr. Rabbit hopped off into the forest with the basket.

"I've lost my tail, but I've gained a basket," he thought. "Maybe I'll find a new tail or something else just as good."

After a while, Mr. Rabbit found a garden. He saw an old woman picking lettuce.

"Oh, please, Mr. Rabbit," she said, "could I borrow your basket to put my lettuce in?"

"If you give me some of your lettuce," replied Mr. Rabbit, "you can keep the basket!" So she did. And off he hopped.

Soon Mr. Rabbit felt hungry. He took a bite of the lettuce. It was delicious!

"I've lost my tail and my basket, but I've found something I like much better!" he thought, feeling happy.

The Magical Locket

It was Princess Crystal's birthday. Her father, the king, had given her a very special present—a beautiful locket.

"This is a magical locket," the king told Princess Crystal. "But it will only work if you say the magic rhyme:

"Magical locket, please listen well,
Help my friend with a kindly spell."

No one knew that, far away in her tower, the wicked witch was watching Princess Crystal's birthday in her crystal ball. When she saw the locket, the witch wanted it for herself.

The next day, Princess Crystal went riding on her favorite horse. She didn't see the witch hiding behind a tree.

As Princess Crystal trotted by, the wicked witch cast her evil spell:

"Frogs and toads, and all things black,
Throw the princess on her back!"

Princess Crystal's horse reared up and threw her to the ground. As quick as a flash, the wicked witch took the locket from around Princess Crystal's neck and threw a net over her.

"Now the locket's mine!" she cackled. She bundled the frightened princess over her shoulder and carried her away.

Soon, they arrived at the witch's tower. A fierce dragon guarded it.

"Don't try to escape, my pretty one," said the witch, "or Horace the dragon will eat you up!"

At the top of the tower, the witch freed Princess Crystal.

"Recognize this?" she asked, holding up the magical locket.

"My locket!" gasped Princess Crystal.

"Yes," hissed the witch. "It's mine now. But I need the magic rhyme to go with it."

"I won't give it to you," said Princess Crystal bravely.

"Then you can stay here until you do!" shouted the witch. "Here's your precious locket," she added, throwing it at Princess Crystal. "It won't do you any good locked in here!"

She stormed out of the room, locking the door behind her.

Princess Crystal felt so alone. She leaned out of the window and began to cry.

Her tears fell on Horace the dragon below.

"You're making me all wet," he said grumpily, flying up to the window. "I'm not crying, even though my wing's broken, and really hurts."

"Oh, you poor thing," said Princess Crystal, feeling sorry for the dragon. "Maybe I can help you." She closed her eyes, held the locket and said the magic rhyme:

"Magical locket, please listen well,
Help my friend with a kindly spell."

Princess Crystal opened her eyes and saw that Horace's wing had completely healed.

"Oh, thank you," he said happily. "My wing is healed, and I don't feel grumpy anymore. But what can I do to return your kindness?"

"Fly and find Prince Robert as quickly as you can," she said.

Horace promised he'd go quickly and, beating his wings, he rose into the air. Soon, Horace found Prince Robert. When he heard that Princess Crystal had been captured by the witch, he jumped onto Horace's back and flew to the rescue.

"Thank goodness Horace found you," cried Princess Crystal as Prince Robert climbed in through the window. But before they could escape, the door opened.

There stood the wicked witch.

"How nice of you to join us, young man," she cackled. "And how handsome you are! But I think you'd look much better as a … *frog!*"

She began to cast an evil spell.

"Oh no," thought Princess Crystal. "I'd better do something." She closed her eyes, held the locket, and whispered the magic rhyme:

"Magical locket, please listen well,
Help my friend with a kindly spell."

When Princess Crystal opened her eyes, the locket's magic had worked. The witch's spell had backfired, and turned her into a frog instead!

"Well done, Princess Crystal!" said Prince Robert.

"Frogspawn and slime!" croaked the frog, then hopped out of the window and was never seen again.

And Princess Crystal, Prince Robert, and Horace the dragon lived happily ever after.

Grandmother Cedar Tree

Once, there lived a large grandmother cedar tree named Seedla. She was tall and strong, but she was sad and lonely.

The Sky God felt sorry for Seedla. He told the warm and gentle South Wind to plant a baby cedar tree next to the grandmother tree.

Seedla was overjoyed, and she adopted the baby cedar tree as her grandson.

As the little tree grew, he sprouted fresh, tender branches. Soon, animals came to nibble on them, and the little tree struggled to grow bigger.

So Seedla moved her long, old branches back and forth to scare the animals away. And the little tree began to grow taller and stronger.

Sometimes, when the cold and wintry North Wind blew extra hard, the little tree felt that his thin branches would bend and break.

So Seedla put her long, strong arms around her grandson to protect him from the North Wind. Then the little tree grew some more.

Sometimes the sun was so strong that it scorched the little tree. So Seedla raised her branches high enough to shade her grandson. And the little tree kept growing.

In time, Seedla's grandson became tall and straight. Many seasons passed. Grandmother Seedla became old and tired. Her grandson, who was now large and strong, felt her sorrow.

"Grandmother, remember when the animals nibbled on me, how you moved your strong branches to protect me?" he said to her. "Well, I have long arms now. I will move them back and forth to scare the animals away as you did.

"And Grandmother, do you not remember when I was small and thin, and the North Wind blew so strongly that I thought I would break, how you put your arms around me to keep me from breaking? My arms are strong now, and I can keep you from bending and breaking.

"And Grandmother, remember when the sun scorched my branches, you lifted your branches high to shade me? Well, now I can lift my long arms to shade you.

"As you took care of me, now I will take care of you."

The grandmother tree smiled gratefully at her grandson, and the two stood side by side for many more seasons.

Puss in the Pantry

Hie, hie, says Anthony,
Puss is in the pantry,
Gnawing, gnawing,
A mutton, mutton bone;
See how she tumbles it,
See how she mumbles it,
See how she tosses
The mutton, mutton bone.

Pussycat, Pussycat

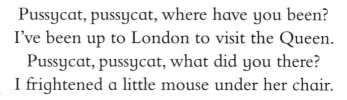

Pussycat, pussycat, where have you been?
I've been up to London to visit the Queen.
Pussycat, pussycat, what did you there?
I frightened a little mouse under her chair.

Pussycat Ate the Dumplings

Pussycat ate the dumplings,
Pussycat ate the dumplings,
Mamma stood by,
And cried, "Oh fie!
Why did you eat the dumplings?"

Sing, Sing

Sing, sing,
What shall I sing?
The cat's run away
With the pudding string!
Do, do,
What shall I do?
The cat's run away
With the pudding too!

Jack Sprat's Cat

Jack Sprat
Had a cat,
It had but one ear;
It went to buy butter
When butter was dear.

A Cat Came Fiddling

A cat came fiddling out of a barn,
With a pair of bagpipes under her arm;
She could sing nothing but, "Fiddle cum fee,
The mouse has married the bumble-bee."
Pipe, cat—dance, mouse,
We'll have a wedding at our good house.

Alfie and Alice

Alfie and Alice were best friends. They went everywhere together. Alfie loved Alice. He thought she was the kindest owner a dog could have. Alice loved Alfie. She thought he was the cutest dog in the whole wide world.

And Alfie and Alice both LOVED their food. Whenever a delicious food smell wafted near Alice's little button nose and Alfie's shiny black nose, the pair of them would dash off to follow the scent.

One day, Alice and Alfie were playing hide-and-seek in the park. Alfie was hiding, but Alice couldn't find him anywhere.

Alice called and called, but Alfie didn't come bounding over as he usually did.

"Try not to worry, Alice," said Mom, gently. "I'm sure he can't have gone far."

Alice wiped away her tears and sniffed the air.

Suddenly, she had a great idea.

"Mom," she cried excitedly. "I know how we can find Alfie. We've got to follow the food smells!"

Mom grinned. "Of course! Alfie LOVES his food."

"And I can smell pizza," shouted Alice. "Come on, let's go!" She rushed off toward the small café by the duck pond.

"Have you seen a little brown dog with black patches?" Alice called out to the café owner.

"Oh, I think he went that way," said the man, and he pointed toward the bandstand.

"This way, Mom," said Alice. "I smell sausages!"

Alice and her mom followed the delicious smell wafting across the grass. When they reached the bandstand, they could see a group of musicians huddled around a smoking barbecue, cooking their lunch.

"Have you seen a little brown—" Alice started to say. But then she saw something …

"Alfie!" Alice cried. There, in the middle of the group, sat Alice's dog. He was eating from a plate of sizzling sausages.

Alice hugged Alfie tightly.

"Don't ever disappear again!" she scolded. "Now, let me have one of those sausages. Yum!"

Moon Stars

It was bedtime. The sun was setting, the owls were swooping overhead, and the squirrels and rabbits were curling up and going to sleep. But Mommy Bear was wide awake. She couldn't find Baby Bear anywhere. He wasn't in the kitchen, eating an extra cookie. He wasn't in the bathroom, brushing his teeth. He wasn't in his bedroom, putting on his pajamas.

"Baby Bear!" she called. "Where are you?"

But there was no reply.

Mommy Bear went out into the woods to look for him. The night animals were out and about. Freddy Bat was hanging upside down from a tree.

"Have you seen my Baby Bear?" she asked.

Freddy Bat gave a few sleepy blinks.

"No, sorry," he replied, yawning. "I've only just woken up."

Mommy Bear walked on past the babbling stream. Billy Fox was drinking some cool water.

"Have you seen my Baby Bear?" she asked.

Billy Fox looked up and shook his head.

"No, I'm afraid not," he said. "I've been eating my breakfast."

So Mommy Bear went farther into the woods until she reached a little clearing. There she saw Ella Badger rolling around in the leaves.

"Have you seen my Baby Bear?" she asked.

Ella Badger thought for a moment. Then she smiled.

"I think I have," she said. "There's a fluffy little bear sitting on the top of the highest hill. I saw him when I was practicing my somersaults."

When Mommy Bear reached the highest hill, she rubbed her eyes in astonishment. Baby Bear had the moon in his lap!

"It fell out of the sky," said Baby Bear. "It landed right in my arms. How can I put it back in the sky, Mommy?"

Mommy Bear sat down next to Baby Bear and snuggled up.

"Well," she said. "Let's think. We could use sticky tape."

"Sticky tape might not be strong enough," said Baby Bear. "How about glue?"

"What if it makes the moon too messy?" said Mommy Bear. "We could bounce it back into the sky like a ball."

Baby shook his head.

"It might break instead of bouncing," he said. "I don't want to go to bed until we know what to do with the moon. How can we put it back where it belongs?"

"Let me have a look," said Mommy Bear. She sniffed the moon. She walked all the way around it. Then she smiled.

"I've got an idea," she said. "This moon looks bigger than normal. I think that it's fallen out of the sky because it grew too big and heavy, and the sky couldn't hold it up anymore!"

Baby Bear opened his eyes very wide.

"How can we make it lighter?" he asked.

"Well," said Mommy Bear, "what we have to do is trim around the edges."

"What will happen then?" asked Baby Bear.

"Let's find out," said his mommy. She took out her nail scissors and trimmed a little bit from all around the moon. Snip! Snip! Snip! And the pieces fell to the ground. Then Mommy Bear cut the pieces into star shapes to take home.

"Now," she said, "let go of the moon."

So Baby Bear did, and the moon floated back up into the sky, until it was high above their heads.

Then Mommy Bear and Baby Bear walked home.

Baby Bear climbed into bed, while Mommy Bear stuck the tiny stars all over the walls. Then she cuddled into bed beside him, and they drifted off to sleep in the golden light of the moon stars.

Thaw

Over the land freckled with snow half-thawed
The speculating rooks at their nests cawed,
And saw from elm-tops, delicate as flower of grass,
What we below could not see, winter pass.

Sunshine

A sunshiny shower
Won't last half an hour.

The Grand Old Duke of York

The grand old Duke of York,
He had ten thousand men.
He marched them up to the top of the hill,
And he marched them down again.
When they were up, they were up,
And when they were down, they were down.
And when they were only halfway up,
They were neither up nor down.

Little Boy Blue

Little Boy Blue, come blow your horn,
The sheep's in the meadow,
The cow's in the corn.
Where is the boy who looks after the sheep?
He's under a haystack fast asleep.
Will you wake him?
No, not I,
For if I do he's sure to cry.

Billy and Me

One, two, three,
I love coffee,
And Billy loves tea,
How good you be.
One two three,
I love coffee,
And Billy loves tea.

Little Nag

I had a little nag
That trotted up and down;
I bridled him, and saddled him,
And trotted out of town.

Bedtime Adventure

Leah and Megan were not only twin sisters—they were best friends, and they played together all day long.

At bedtime, the twins couldn't wait to wake up and have more fun again in the morning.

One night, as Leah settled down on the top bunk bed, she made a wish upon a star.

"I wish we could play together in our sleep, too," she whispered.

That night, Leah was dreaming of playing with mermaids when, suddenly, she saw Megan flying around the room.

"Are you really flying?" Leah asked, rubbing her eyes.

"Yes," said Megan with a grin. "Come and play!"

Leah jumped out of bed and floated up to the ceiling. Megan took her hand and the window opened, as if by magic.

Together the twins flew out into the sky.

The sisters slid down some moonbeams and dove into the sea. They swam underwater with some fish, while mermaids with silvery tails darted along beside them.

"Let's be mermaids, too," said Leah.

Their legs started to sparkle until they turned into mermaid tails. Leah and Megan flicked and twisted their tails as they followed the mermaids to a big rock. Then they all pulled themselves onto the rock. They ran gem-encrusted combs through their hair, and sang beautiful songs that made dolphins dance in the water below.

Slowly, the stars faded and the sky grew brighter. The night was nearly over … and it was time for the sisters to go home.

Leah opened her eyes and looked down at Megan, who was grinning up at her from the bottom bunk bed.

"Was it all just a dream?" she asked in a whisper.

"Of course," said Megan. "But we both remember it, and I can't wait for our next bedtime adventure!"

My Little Puppy

Everyone agreed that Isobel's little puppy, Patches, looked adorable. He had stumpy legs and a round, chubby tummy, silky-soft ears, lively brown eyes, and a small patch just over his right eye.

Isobel loved Patches, and Patches loved Isobel.

The only problem was that Patches was always getting himself—and Isobel—into trouble. Lots of trouble!

On Monday, Patches chewed one of Dad's slippers … and the strap on Mom's new purse.

"Can't that animal chew on his toy?" complained Dad.

"He doesn't like it," sighed Isobel, trying to give Patches the rubber bone she had bought for him.

Patches put his paws on Isobel's hands and licked them.

"That tickles," giggled Isobel. It was impossible to be cross with Patches for long.

On Tuesday, Patches pulled the clothes off the laundry line and dragged them across the ground. The clothes were all dirty.

"Oh, Patches, not again!" complained Dad.

"He was only trying to play," defended Isobel. "He's really sorry, aren't you, Patches?" Patches barked and rolled over on his back, waving his legs in the air. Even Dad had to laugh.

On Wednesday, Patches knocked over a vase.

"He was only trying to smell the flowers," said Isobel.

Patches put his head to one side and barked softly.

"See," said Isobel. "He's saying 'sorry,' aren't you, Patches?"

Mom grinned. "All right, but be more careful!"

Later that day, Mrs. May, who lived next door, was in her backyard. Her white cat, Snowy, jumped on top of the fence and hissed at Patches.

Patches barked back.

"Please don't let that naughty puppy frighten poor Snowy," called Mrs. May.

"We'll make sure Patches stays out of Snowy's way," said Mom.

"Yes, please do," sniffed Mrs. May. "Poor Snowy!"

"Poor Snowy, indeed," muttered Isobel. "That cat is always teasing Patches."

"Now, now, Isobel," soothed Mom. "Mrs. May was telling me earlier that she's lost her gold ring. I think her husband gave it to her a long time ago. She's very upset about it, and that probably makes her seem more cross than she really is. And you know she loves Snowy as much as you love Patches."

Mom was right. Mrs. May and Snowy were best friends.

The next day, Isobel and Patches were in the garden with Mom and Dad when Mrs. May came out of her house.

"Any sign of your ring?" called Mom.

Mrs May shook her head sadly.

"I think I've lost it for good," she said.

Just then, Snowy jumped down from the fence, scratched Patches across his nose with her paw, then ran off.

"Snowykins!" cried Mrs. May. "Naughty kitty!"

Patches squeezed through a hole in the fence and began to chase Snowy around and around Mrs. May's yard.

Isobel and her parents followed. Around and around they went, until Dad caught Patches.

"Oh no! Look at my vegetables!" cried Mrs. May. "And my poor flowers!"

"We're so sorry," said Isobel's mom. "We'll help you replant them."

"That would be very kind," said Mrs. May.

Mom and Mrs. May picked up the plant pots and the gardening tools. Dad tied together the runner-bean canes that had been knocked over. And Isobel and Patches dug holes to put back some of the flowers that had been disturbed.

"What's that, Patches?" asked Isobel, as Patches pushed a lump of soil toward her with his nose. Isobel scraped away the soil, then leaped to her feet.

"Mrs. May! Mrs. May! Patches has found your ring!"

Mrs. May was delighted. "Oh, you clever puppy!" she said, patting Patches' head. "How can I ever thank you?"

And after that, Isobel, Patches, and Mrs. May were the best of friends.

Even though Patches still sometimes chased naughty Snowy around and around the yard!

Mia's Rainbows

It was the perfect day for rainbows, and Mia wished she could play outside in the rain and sunshine with all her friends. But she was feeling sick. So her mommy tucked her into bed with an electric blanket and a book.

"If only I could see a rainbow," she told her mommy.

Mia's mommy felt sorry for Mia. Then she had an idea. She invited all Mia's friends over and gave them each a tin of paint and a paintbrush. As soon as Mia fell asleep, they tiptoed into her room. Swish! Swoosh! They carefully painted every wall and even the ceiling, filling her room with bright rainbows. When Mia woke up and saw them, a huge smile spread over her face.

"I love rainbows!" she said. "My amazing friends have made me feel better already!"

Jungle Shower

Grace the elephant loved showering under the biggest waterfall in the jungle. She splashed and sang at the top of her voice. But the other animals wanted a peaceful shower time.

"Stop singing!" shouted the monkeys.

"Stop splashing!" squealed the parrots.

"But shower time should be fun," said Grace. She felt sad that the others weren't having a good time. Then she had an idea.

"Everyone loves bubbles," she said. "I'll make shower time so much fun that they *have* to enjoy it!"

She put her trunk in the water, then lifted it up to the sky … and *blew*! Bubbles rose and danced on the breeze, popping around the animals. The monkeys, parrots, giraffes, and everyone else started to smile. Soon the jungle was filled with bubbles and the sound of Grace's singing— and everyone joined in!

The Enormous Pancake

Once upon a time, there was a woman who had seven little boys. They were always hungry.

"If you are very good," said their mother, "I will make you the biggest pancake you have ever seen!"

So she cracked the eggs, measured the milk, weighed the flour, and mixed it all together. Then she poured the mixture into a hot pan. The pancake was going to be enormous!

When it was time to flip it over, the hungry little boys cried out, "Toss it in the air, Mother, please!"

So their mother tossed the pancake high into the air.

But the pancake didn't want to be eaten, so with a flip and a flop it landed on the floor and rolled out of the door.

"Stop!" cried the hungry little boys. "We want to eat you!"

But the pancake didn't want to be eaten. So it rolled down the road, with the boys and their mother chasing after it.

Soon, the pancake passed a cat.

"Stop!" meowed the cat, licking her lips. "You would taste yummy washed down with a bowl of milk. Let me eat you."

But the pancake just rolled faster. "Seven little boys and their mother couldn't catch me, and you won't either!" it shouted. So the cat chased after it.

194

Next, the pancake passed a duck pond.

"Stop!" quacked the duck. "I prefer pancakes to stale bread, so I'm going to eat you up!"

But the pancake rolled even faster. "Seven little boys, their mother, and a cat couldn't catch me, and you won't either!" So the duck chased after it.

Then, the pancake passed a cow in a field.

"Stop!" mooed the cow. "I'll eat you instead of this grass!"

But the pancake rolled even faster still. "Seven little boys, their mother, a cat, and a duck couldn't catch me, and you won't either!" So the cow chased after it.

Soon, the pancake met a pig by a river.

"Can you help me cross the river?" asked the pancake.

"Of course!" snorted the pig. "Sit on my nose, and I'll carry you across." So the pancake jumped onto his nose.

In a flash, the pig flipped the pancake into the air and gobbled it up in one enormous GULP! "Yum!" said the pig.

Just then, the seven little boys, their mother, the cat, the duck, and the cow arrived.

"Have you seen an enormous pancake?" they asked.

"Yes," snorted the pig happily, "and it was delicious!"

Sleeping Beauty

Once upon a time, a king and queen had a beautiful baby girl. The proud parents decided to hold a christening feast to celebrate, so they invited kings, queens, princes, and princesses from other kingdoms.

Five good fairies lived in the kingdom, and the king wanted them to be godmothers to his daughter. One of these fairies was very old, and no one had seen her in years or even knew where she was. So when the king sent out the invitations, he invited only the four young fairies.

The day of the christening arrived, and the palace was full of laughter and dancing.

After the delicious feast, the four fairies gave the princess their magical gifts.

The first fairy waved her wand over the crib and said, "You shall be kind and considerate."

The second fairy said, "You shall be beautiful and loving."

The third fairy said, "You shall be clever and thoughtful…."

Suddenly, the palace doors flew open. It was the old fairy. She was furious because she hadn't been invited to the feast.

She flew up to the crib and waved her wand over the princess.

"One day, the king's daughter shall prick her finger on a spindle and fall down dead!" she screeched, and then rushed out.

"I cannot undo the spell," said the fourth fairy, "but I can soften it. The princess will prick her finger on a spindle, but she will not die. Instead, the princess and everyone within the palace and its grounds will fall into a deep sleep for one hundred years."

The king thanked the fairy and then, to protect his daughter, ordered every spindle in the kingdom to be burned.

The years passed, and the princess grew into a beautiful, clever, and kind young woman.

One day, the princess decided to explore some rooms in the palace she had never been in before. After a while, she came to a little door at the top of a tall tower. Inside, there was an old woman working at her spinning wheel. The princess didn't know that the woman was really the old fairy in disguise.

"What are you doing?" the princess asked curiously.

"I'm spinning thread, dear," replied the woman.

"Can I try?" asked the princess.

No sooner had she touched the spindle than she pricked her finger and fell into a deep sleep.

As she fell asleep, every living thing within the castle walls fell into a deep sleep too.

As time passed, a hedge of thorns sprang up around the palace. It grew higher and thicker every year, until only the tallest towers could be seen above it.

The story of the beautiful princess who lay sleeping within its walls spread throughout the land. She became known as Sleeping Beauty. Many princes tried to break through the thorns to rescue Sleeping Beauty, but none were successful.

Exactly one hundred years after the princess had fallen asleep, a handsome prince, having heard the story of Sleeping Beauty, decided to try and awaken the sleeping princess.

The prince didn't know that the fairy's spell was coming to its end. As he pushed against the thick hedge, every thorn turned into a beautiful rose, and a path magically formed to let him pass.

Soon the prince arrived at the palace. He saw people and animals asleep in every room.

At last he found the tiny room in the tower where Sleeping Beauty lay. He kissed her gently.

The sleeping princess opened her eyes and smiled. With that one look, they fell in love.

All around the palace, people started waking up. The spell had been broken!

The king called for a huge wedding feast to be prepared, and this time he invited every person, and fairy, in the entire kingdom.

Sleeping Beauty married her handsome prince, and they lived happily ever after.

Roses Are Red

Roses are red,
Violets are blue,
Sugar is sweet,
And so are you.

Little Poll Parrot

Little Poll Parrot
Sat in his garret,
Eating toast and tea;
A little brown mouse
Jumped into the house,
And stole it all away.

Little Bo-Peep

Little Bo-Peep
Has lost her sheep,
And she doesn't know
Where to find them.
Leave them alone,
And they'll come home,
Wagging their tails
Behind them.

Small is the Wren

Small is the wren,
Black is the rook,
Great is the sinner
That steals this book.

The Legacy

My father died a month ago
And left me all his riches:
A feather bed, a wooden leg,
And a pair of leather britches,
A coffee pot without a spout,
And a cup without a handle,
A casserole dish without a lid,
And half a farthing candle.

Sowing Corn

One for the mouse,
One for the crow,
One to rot,
One to grow.

The Wild Swans

Once upon a time, in a distant land, there lived a king. He was blessed with eleven sons and one daughter, Elisa. Sadly, his wife had died. But the king was a loving father, and the children were happy.

One day, however, everything changed. The king decided to marry again. His new wife was cruel, but the king was blind to her evil ways. She had Elisa sent away to live with a poor family in the forest, and the princes banished from the kingdom. She cast an enchantment on the boys, transforming them into wild swans. They flew away, wondering sadly if they would ever see their sister again.

The years passed. Elisa was never allowed to return home, and every day her heart ached to see her brothers again.

On her fifteenth birthday, she decided to go in search of the princes.

Elisa walked through the forest until she reached the shores of the ocean. As she gazed at the sun setting below the sea, eleven wild swans landed on the sand. Elisa gasped as the swans suddenly transformed into her brothers.

"Whenever the sun is up, we live as swans," the eldest brother explained. "Only at nightfall may we return to our human form. We live across the ocean now, far away. Come home with us."

So Elisa went to live with her swan brothers.

One night, she had a strange dream. A fairy told her that she must make a shirt made of nettles for each brother. Once they put it on, the spell would be broken and they would be men again. But Elisa was to stay silent until her work was finished, otherwise her brothers would die.

When Elisa awoke, she started on her task right away.
She didn't utter a word, even though the nettles stung her
hands. She worked hard all day. Just as she was about to return
to her brothers, a group of huntsmen, led by a king, appeared.

The king fell in love with Elisa at first sight.

"Come with me to my palace and be my queen," he said.

As Elisa was sworn to silence,
she couldn't protest.

Holding the nettle shirts,
she reluctantly left
with the king.

"Your Majesty, you cannot marry this girl," the archbishop complained. "There is witchcraft at work here, mark my words!"

That night, Elisa tried to sneak out of the palace, but the archbishop caught her and brought her before the king.

"The girl is up to something, Your Majesty," cried the archbishop. "She is a witch!"

The king was heartbroken. Elisa dared not speak to defend herself, and so she was condemned to death.

At sunrise, still clutching the nettle shirts, Elisa was taken to her place of execution. Suddenly, eleven swans swooped down from the sky. Elisa threw the shirts over her swan brothers. They instantly changed into young men.

"Now I may speak," Elisa exclaimed. "I am no witch. All I ever wanted was to break an evil curse and free my brothers."

The king was shocked by this.

"My true love," he cried. "Can you ever forgive me?"

Elisa nodded. The spell had been broken. She had her brothers back, and she knew she would never be unhappy again.

Stuck on the Moon

Every night, when the moon and the stars were out and the children had gone to bed, the pages of the nursery rhyme book started to flutter. The characters clambered out, then played and sang together.

But, one night, the cow who jumped over the moon didn't jump over the moon. She got stuck! Everyone looked up at the cow, stuck on the moon.

"Oh dear," said Itsby Bitsy spider. "That wasn't supposed to happen."

"We have to get her down before the children wake up," said Jack Sprat. "We can't have anyone missing from the book."

Luckily, Humpty Dumpty had an idea.

"Let's stand on each other's shoulders," he said. "We can reach the moon and help the cow get down."

So one by one, they clambered onto each other's shoulders. The three little pigs stood on the book, the crooked man stood on the three little pigs, the owl stood on the dish, and so on. It took a long time, but at last the wibbling, wobbling ladder of characters reached almost up to the shining moon. Almost....

"Who's missing?" cried Little Bo-Peep.

Suddenly, they all heard a loud crash. One of the five little monkeys had been playing with a ball of wool, and had pushed it right out of the book!

"Little monkey, come on!" they shouted. So the monkey clambered above his brothers and sisters, and all the way to the top of the swaying ladder. He helped the cow down, and then everyone ran back to their places in the book, just in time, before the children started to open their eyes!

Crocodile Teeth

Chloe Crocodile was getting ready for bedtime. "Will the Tooth Fairy come tonight?" she asked her mommy.

"Your tooth hasn't fallen out yet," her mommy replied, and she kissed Chloe goodnight.

As Chloe lay by the creek, she wobbled her tooth, but it wouldn't budge. Would it ever fall out? Suddenly, a tiny fairy fluttered out from behind a leaf and landed on Chloe's nose.

"I'm Kitty the Tooth Fairy," she said. "Can I help?"

Chloe's mouth fell open in surprise. Kitty reached in and gave the tooth an expert twist and—presto! It was out! Kitty put it into her pocket.

"This deserves a very special coin indeed," said Kitty. "Look under your pillow in the morning."

Then Kitty said goodbye and fluttered away as quickly as she had appeared.

The next day, Chloe found a crocodile coin under her pillow, with a little note that said: "Even crocodiles have visits from the Tooth Fairy." Chloe couldn't wait to show her mommy!

London Bells

Merry go up and merry go down,
To ring the bells of London town.
Halfpence and farthings,
Say the bells of St. Martin's.
Pancakes and fritters,
Say the bells of St. Peter's.
Two sticks and an apple,
Say the bells of Whitechapel.

For Every Evil Under the Sun

For every evil under the sun,
There is a remedy, or there is none.
If there be one, try and find it;
If there be none, never mind it.

Went into My Grandmother's Garden

I went into my grandmother's garden,
And there I found a farthing.
I went into my next door neighbor's;
There I bought
A pipkin and a popkin,
A slipkin and a slopkin,
A nailboard, a sailboard,
And all for a farthing.

Fairy Friends Forever

Deep in the woods, poor Eloise the fairy was trapped under a nutshell that had fallen from a tree. Try as she might, it was just too heavy for her to move.

Then suddenly, the nutshell lifted and a little girl gazed down at her.

Eloise was scared of humans, but the girl looked kind.

"Thank you," she said. "What's your name?"

"Matilda," whispered the girl. "Are you really a fairy?"

Suddenly, Eloise had an idea. She waved her wand and shrank Matilda to fairy size.

"Come to Fairyland and find out!" she said.

Eloise showed Matilda all around her magical home. They had tea in her toadstool house and gathered dewberries in the Fairyland Forest. They giggled and shared secrets, and soon they felt as if they had always known each other.

Then it was time for Matilda to go home. Eloise gave her a tiny Fairyland flower.

"I'll never forget you," she whispered.

"And I won't forget you," promised Matilda, as they linked their little fingers together. "Fairy friends forever!"

Winter Snowdrops

One winter's day, a fairy named Snowdrop was sitting in a tree when she heard someone crying. She fluttered down and saw a girl sitting among the tree roots.

"What's wrong, little girl?" Snowdrop asked.

"I can't find any flowers for my mother's birthday," sobbed the girl.

Snowdrop felt sorry for her.

"Fetch me the smoothest pebble you can find," she said. "Then bury it under the tree."

The little girl searched and searched, and finally found a pebble as smooth as silk. She buried it as she'd been told, and patted the soil down. Then Snowdrop waved her wand, and tiny plant shoots poked through the soil and started to grow. They rose higher and higher, until they burst into brilliant white snowdrops.

"Thank you!" said the little girl, picking the flowers. "Mommy will love them."

The little girl never saw Snowdrop again. But every year, on the girl's mother's birthday, Snowdrop secretly used her magic, and there was always a patch of bright snowdrops waiting for her to pick!

The Wedding

Pussycat, wussicat, with a white foot,
When is your wedding, and I'll come to it.
The beer's to brew, and the bread's to bake,
Pussycat, wussicat, don't be too late.

First

First in a carriage,
Second in a gig,
Third on a donkey,
And fourth on a pig.

Humpty Dumpty

Humpty Dumpty
Sat on a wall,
Humpty Dumpty
Had a great fall.
All the king's horses
And all the king's men,
Couldn't put Humpty
Together again!

Slowly, Slowly

Slowly, slowly, very slowly
Creeps the garden snail.
Slowly, slowly, very slowly
Up the garden rail.

Quickly, quickly, very quickly
Runs the little mouse.
Quickly, quickly, very quickly
Round about the house.

Hark! Hark!

Hark, hark,
The dogs do bark,
Beggars are coming to town:
Some in rags,
Some in tags,
And some in velvet gowns.

This Little Bird

This little bird flaps its wings,
Flaps its wings, flaps its wings,
This little bird flaps its wings,
And flies away in the morning!

Wherever You Go... I Go

The sun comes up and smiles on us
And starts to warm the early day.
My sleepy eyes can see you move.
Wherever you go ... I go.

Then out we dash, to leap and play
And scramble in the morning sun.
You push some leaves aside for me ...

(Hey Mom! Hey, look!
Guess who's a tree?!)
Let's go have fun, and mess about.
Whenever you play ... I play.

(Oh no!)
The skies turn gray,
It starts to rain
And you just want to keep me dry ...
(Thanks Mom!)
I run and shelter under you.
Wherever you are ... I am.

And as we walk on, trunk in trunk
And talk about the things I'll do ...
(You'll teach me, Mom ...
you always do.)
You tell me just how much you care,
(I love you Mom, I sing to you!)
Whatever you love ... I love.

Then when it's time to scrub me clean,
We'll splish and splosh and splash about.
You wash away my bathtime fears,
(Just don't forget behind my ears!)
Whenever you smile ... I smile.

And when the day has reached its end
And both of us are getting tired,
I'll snuggle up and feel your warmth.
Whenever you sleep ... I sleep.

Three Little Kittens

Three little kittens,
They lost their mittens,
And they began to cry,
"Oh, mother dear. We sadly fear
Our mittens we have lost."

"What? Lost your mittens,
You naughty kittens!
Then you shall have no pie.
Meow, meow, meow, meow.
No, you shall have no pie."

The three little kittens,
They found their mittens,
And they began to smile,
"Oh, mother dear. See here, see here,
Our mittens we have found."

"What? Found your mittens,
You clever kittens!
Then you shall have some pie.
Purr, purr, purr, purr.
Oh, let us have some pie."

Mother Hubbard

Old Mother Hubbard went to the cupboard
To get her poor doggy a bone;
But when she came there the cupboard was bare,
And so the poor doggy had none.

She went to the tailor's
To buy him a coat,
But when she came back
He was riding a goat.

She went to the cobbler's
To buy him some shoes,
But when she came back
He was reading the news.

She went to the hosier's
To buy him some hose,
But when she came back
He was dressed in his clothes.

The dame made a curtsey,
The dog made a bow,
The dame said, "Your servant,"
The dog said, "Bow wow."

Cleo and the Unicorn

Cleo dreamed of meeting a unicorn.

"They don't exist," said Cleo's mom.

"You're being silly," said her brother.

Even her dad smiled and patted her on the head.

One day, Cleo was playing in the yard when she heard a snorting noise behind the toolshed. She went to find out what it was and saw a small, muddy animal.

"Hello," said Cleo in a gentle voice. "What are you?" She carefully picked up the creature. "You're a tiny pony!" she exclaimed. "Let me clean you up, little one."

Cleo bathed the pony in her wading pool. Underneath all the dirt, the pony was as white as snow. Cleo wrapped it in her best fleecy blanket and read it a story until it fell asleep. Then she looked up and gasped in surprise. A shining white unicorn was standing beside the shed!

"I've always wanted to see a unicorn," whispered Cleo.

"You already have," said the unicorn with a smile. "You are cuddling my baby. I have been searching for him all day."

"But he doesn't have a horn," said Cleo.

"Unicorn horns don't grow until we're older," said the unicorn. "Thank you for taking care of him."

Cleo unfolded the blanket, and the little unicorn woke up. He trotted happily to his mommy.

"Will I ever see him again?" Cleo asked.

"Because you took care of my baby, a tiny bit of unicorn magic will stay with you," the unicorn said. "If you are ever in trouble, we will come to help you."

"Thank you," gasped Cleo happily.

The unicorn flicked her mane, and left in a swirl of silver sparkles. Cleo couldn't stop smiling. She had met a real unicorn, and found that wishes *do* come true.

Androclus and the Lion

A long time ago in Rome, there lived a poor slave whose name was Androclus. His master was a cruel man, and Androclus wished that he could be free.

One night, Androclus managed to escape. He ran away and hid in a cave outside the city.

Androclus was so tired, cold, and hungry that he fell into a deep sleep. A while later, a great noise woke him up. A lion had come into the cave and was roaring loudly. At first, Androclus feared that the lion would eat him. But then he realized that the lion was limping in pain.

Boldly, Androclus took the lion's paw in his hand to see what was wrong. A large thorn was poking out of the lion's pad. Androclus removed the thorn gently. The lion was so grateful that he licked Androclus' face!

After this, Androclus and the lion became the best of friends and lived happily together in the cave.

Several months later, some soldiers were passing nearby. They found Androclus and took him back to Rome.

At that time, it was the law that any slave who'd run away, and was caught, had to fight a hungry lion for their freedom.

Poor Androclus was put in an arena to await his fate. He closed his eyes in fear as a hungry lion ran toward him. But instead of being attacked, the lion licked Androclus' face!

Androclus gave a cry of joy. It was his old friend the lion from the cave. He put his arms around the huge beast and hugged it in gratitude.

The crowd was astounded—they had never seen anything like this before. They called out to Androclus to explain what had happened.

"I am a man," Androclus cried. "But no man has ever been kind to me. This magnificent lion is the closest thing I've ever had to a friend. We love each other like brothers."

The crowd was so moved by Androclus' story that they chanted, "Let him live and be free! And let the lion go, too!"

And from then on, Androclus and the lion lived happily together in Rome.

For Want of a Nail

For want of a nail, the shoe was lost;
For want of the shoe, the horse was lost;
For want of the horse, the rider was lost;
For want of the rider, the battle was lost;
For want of the battle, the kingdom was lost;
And all for the want of a horseshoe nail.

Pease Porridge

Pease porridge hot,
Pease porridge cold,
Pease porridge in the pot,
Nine days old.
Some like it hot,
Some like it cold,
Some like it in the pot,
Nine days old.

Jack Sprat

Jack Sprat could eat no fat,
His wife could eat no lean,
And so between the two of them
They licked the platter clean.

I Scream

I scream, you scream,
We all scream for ice cream!

Old Joe Brown

Old Joe Brown, he had a wife,
She was all of eight feet tall.
She slept with her head in the kitchen,
And her feet stuck out in the hall.

I Met a Man

As I was going up the stair
I met a man who wasn't there.
He wasn't there again today—
Oh! How I wish he'd go away!

The Morning and the Evening Star

Once upon a time, there were two stars who were the sons of the Golden King of the Heavens. The two brothers were called Tschen and Shen. They loved each other very much, but they were always quarreling.

One evening, they started arguing as usual.

"I shine brighter than you," mocked Shen.

"No you don't!" roared Tschen. "I can twinkle all night!" And he struck Shen a terrible blow.

Both stars were so angry, they made a vow, there and then, that they would never look upon each other again.

Their father tried to help them make friends, but the brothers would not listen.

So now, Tschen only appears in the evening as the Evening Star. And Shen only appears in the morning as the Morning Star, once Tschen has disappeared from sight. The two stars never appear together, but their father continues to try to get them to make peace with each other.

The Moon Lake

A terrible drought came to the jungle, and the elephants' watering hole dried up. They traveled to another lake on the other side of the jungle. On the way, they passed through a colony of rabbits. Hundreds of rabbits were injured under the herd's big stomping feet.

"We must stop the elephants from passing through here again," shouted the rabbit king, and he went to ask the elephant king to meet him at the lake.

There, the two kings saw the Moon reflected in the still water.

"I have a message from the Moon," said the rabbit king. "You have soiled his lake. You must leave, or something terrible will happen to your herd."

"I'm so sorry," cried the elephant king. As he bowed down, his trunk rippled the water. The Moon seemed to move.

"Now the Moon is angrier than ever," said the rabbit king. "You have touched the sacred water of his lake."

"Oh, please forgive me!" wept the elephant king. "We will never come here again." And the elephants went away. It never occurred to them that the clever little rabbit had tricked them!

Princess Elodie's Wish Hunt

Princess Elodie lived in Cloudland, and every day she chose which one of her beautiful cloud ponies she wanted to ride. Then she galloped around her kingdom to collect the wishes of children who had wished upon a star.

One morning, she found it very hard to decide which pony to ride. Should she choose Locket with her golden mane, or Emerald with her sparkling green eyes? The cloud ponies were all so beautiful. Then she heard a soft whinny and turned around. Behind her was a white pony with a curly mane that was as soft as the clouds.

"Hello, Cobweb," said Princess Elodie. "Would you like to go for a ride this morning?"

Cobweb whinnied again, so Princess Elodie fetched a saddle of blue satin.

"Let's go wish-hunting!" she said.

With Princess Elodie on his back, Cobweb galloped over the fluffy cloud hills and through the soft cloud meadows. Wishes were easy to spot because they looked like flowers, and the cloud bunnies loved to chase them.

Princess Elodie scooped up the wishes and put them in her pocket.

Just then, she spotted something half hidden among the cloud blossoms. After telling Cobweb to wait, she slipped down and brushed the blossoms aside. A little brown teddy bear was lying there, looking very sad.

"Poor lost teddy," said Princess Elodie, cuddling him tightly. "I'll look after you."

Cobweb carried Princess Elodie and the teddy back to the Cloud Palace. After Princess Elodie had removed the blue satin saddle and given Cobweb some food, she took the teddy into the palace. First she mended a tear along his arm, and then she washed him and sat him beside the roaring fire to dry.

"Now," she said. "What shall I do with you?"

She emptied her pockets, and the wishes spilled out over the palace floor. There were wishes for dolls, sunny days, carnivals, and lots more, but Princess Elodie was looking for a very special wish. It took a long time to sort through and grant all the wishes, but at last she found what she was looking for. A lonely little boy had wished for a teddy bear friend.

Smiling, Princess Elodie went to fetch Cobweb. By the time she had brushed him down and saddled him, the teddy was dry. Princess Elodie tucked him under her arm, climbed onto Cobweb and held up the little boy's wish.

"Take us to the child who made this wish, please," she said.

Cobweb neighed and walked to the edge of Cloudland. A puffy cloud started to change shape, forming a set of steps that wound down through the night sky. Cobweb trotted down the cloud steps, while Elodie waved to the stars that twinkled all around them. The steps led them all the way to the little boy's bedroom window.

"Shhh," said Princess Elodie. She slipped off Cobweb's back onto the windowsill. Then she opened the window and stepped inside. The little boy was fast asleep in his bed, so Princess Elodie tucked the teddy into bed beside him. In his sleep, the boy smiled and put his arm around the teddy.

"Time to go," said Princess Elodie.

She climbed out of the window and back onto Cobweb. Then he carried her up to Cloudland, where her swinging bed was hanging from the moon.

Yawning, Princess Elodie took Cobweb's saddle off and gave him a blanket and some food. Then she climbed onto her swing and drifted off to sleep, dreaming of the teddy and his happy new home.

Little Betty Blue

Little Betty Blue
Lost a holiday shoe.
What can little Betty do?
Give her another
To match the other,
And then she may
Swagger in two.

Gilly Silly Jarter

Gilly Silly Jarter,
Who has lost a garter,
In a shower of rain.
The miller found it,
The miller ground it,
And the miller gave it
To Silly again.

Silly Sally

Silly Sally swiftly shooed seven silly sheep.
The seven silly sheep Silly Sally shooed shilly-shallied south.
These sheep shouldn't sleep in a shack;
Sheep should sleep in a shed.

Charley Barley

Charley Barley, butter and eggs,
Sold his wife for three duck eggs.
When the ducks began to lay,
Charley Barley flew away.

Elsie Marley

Elsie Marley's grown so fine,
She won't get up to feed the swine,
But lies in bed till eight or nine,
Lazy Elsie Marley!

Mrs. White

Mrs. White had a fright
In the middle of the night.
She saw a ghost, eating toast,
Halfway up a lamp post.

Little Rabbit's Big Adventure!

Little Rabbit sat still in the tall grass. He glanced all around, but nothing looked familiar. Mommy Rabbit had told him not to go too far from the burrow. But, being a curious little bunny, he'd forgotten her words as soon as he'd seen the little buzzing bee fly by and had decided to follow it. Now he didn't know where he was.

"Oh no! I'm lost," cried Little Rabbit. "How will I get home?"

He looked around again. A beautiful pink butterfly was fluttering around some flowers nearby.

"Hello, Mrs. Butterfly," called Little Rabbit. "I'm lost. Do you know where my burrow is?"

"Sorry, I don't," said the butterfly. "Try asking the sheep in that field."

"That's a good idea," replied Little Rabbit. He hopped off through the flowers and squeezed under a fence.

"Hello, Mrs. Sheep," said Little Rabbit, "do you know where my burrow is?"

"No, I'm sorry, my dear," baaed the sheep.

Tears started to slide down Little Rabbit's face. "I miss my mommy, and I want to go home!"

"Don't cry," a squirrel called out from a tree at the edge of the field. "I know where your burrow is. Follow me."

"Oh, thank you, Mr. Squirrel!" said Little Rabbit.

Little Rabbit followed the squirrel into the woods. After a little while the squirrel stopped.

"Here we are!" he said.

And there was Mommy Rabbit, standing by a small dark hole at the base of a big tree.

"Little Rabbit!" cried Mommy Rabbit, scooping him into her arms. "Where have you been? I've been so worried."

Little Rabbit told Mommy Rabbit all about his big adventure.

"What a brave bunny you are!" said Mommy.

Little Rabbit smiled and snuggled closer to his mommy. "But it's good to be back home."

Sparrow

Little brown sparrow, sat upon a tree,
Way up in the branches, safe as he can be!
Hopping through the green leaves, he will play,
High above the ground is where he will stay.

Little Ginger Cat

Little ginger cat,
Sitting in the sun,
Watching all the birds
Flying just for fun.
Hear them chirp and tweet,
As they fly so free,
Just as if to say,
"You cannot catch me!"

Little Robin Redbreast

Little Robin Redbreast
Sat upon a rail:
Niddle-noddle went his head,
Wiggle-waggle went his tail.

The North Wind Doth Blow

The north wind doth blow,
And we shall have snow,
And what will poor Robin do then?
Poor thing!

He'll sit in a barn,
And to keep himself warm,
Will hide his head under his wing.
Poor thing!

Magpies

One for sorrow, two for joy,
Three for a girl, four for a boy,
Five for silver, six for gold,
Seven for a secret never to be told.

Run, Little Mice

Run, little mice, little mice, run!
Don't let that naughty cat have his fun.
Hide beneath the floor until he's gone away,
And then, little mice, come on out and play!

Daisy and the Genie

Daisy bought an old tin lamp at a rummage sale.

"It just needs a quick polish, and it will look as good as new again," she decided.

But when Daisy rubbed the lamp with a cloth, there was a loud bang and a puff of smoke. A small boy appeared with his arms folded across his chest.

"I am a genie!" he said. "I grant you three wishes!"

"Wow!" said Daisy. "How long have you been in the lamp?"

"I've been trapped for ages," the little genie admitted. "I'm training to be a genie. I was waiting for someone to rub the lamp and say their wishes, so I could return to Genie School."

"Can you really give me three wishes?" Daisy asked.

The genie nodded. "They might go wrong," he warned her. "I'm still learning. That's why I need to go back home."

"I wish for a new swing," Daisy began.

The genie snapped his fingers and a shiny new spring appeared in Daisy's hand.

"Oops!" said the genie. "That wasn't supposed to happen."

"Let's try something else," said Daisy with a laugh. "I wish for a house made of chocolate!"

Once again, the genie snapped his fingers, and a large chocolate mouse appeared in Daisy's other hand.

"Oh dear," said the genie, sadly. "I'm not doing very well."

Daisy felt sorry for the little genie. She tried again.

"I wish for ... a pet dog," she said finally.

The genie snapped his fingers, and a frog appeared in Daisy's pocket. Daisy laughed, then noticed the genie was fading away.

"Where are you going?" she cried.

"I'm going back to Genie School," said the genie. "When a human makes three wishes, I can return. Thank you, Daisy!"

The genie and the lamp disappeared in a puff of smoke. Daisy looked at the spring, the chocolate mouse, and the frog, and she smiled.

"You're welcome," she whispered.

Darcie's Treasure

Darcie's uncle was a treasure hunter. He used a special metal detector to search for riches.

One day, Darcie lost her necklace in the garden. So she asked her uncle if he could help her find it.

"Once, I discovered old coins and a medieval queen's jewelry in your garden," he told Darcie. "Legend says that she left a priceless golden goblet here too, but it's probably just a story."

Then Darcie's uncle showed her how to use the metal detector. When they reached the end of the garden, it beeped. Darcie and her uncle started to dig. They found a dirty old cup. When Darcie washed it, she saw that it was gold with red rubies around the side.

"The queen's goblet!" gasped her uncle.

Then the metal detector beeped again. This time they found Darcie's necklace. "You're going to be the best treasure hunter ever, Darcie!" said her uncle, with a grin.

Magic Museum

Zara loved the costume museum. She was fascinated by the clothes people wore hundreds of years ago, and the things they used in their homes. Best of all, she loved imagining that she lived in the old days too.

One day, during a visit, the guide asked Zara if she'd like to try something on. Feeling excited, Zara dressed up in a kitchen maid's uniform. Suddenly, the room around her disappeared, and she found herself in a kitchen full of busy maids and butlers.

"Hurry up!" shouted the cook. "Don't dawdle!"

At first, Zara helped the cook prepare the food. But soon she was washing dishes and scrubbing floors. It was hard work! As Zara bent down, her cap fell off. And in a twinkling, the servants and the kitchen vanished. Zara was back in the museum.

"Will you come back tomorrow?" asked the guide.

"Yes, please. But I think a princess dress might suit me better!" said Zara, thinking about the kitchen from long ago.

The Clever Monkey

One day, Tiger was prowling through the jungle, looking for his lunch. He was just about to pounce on an unsuspecting deer, when his legs became trapped in a tangle of vines.

Poor Tiger was trying to think of a way to escape the trap, when he saw the deer he'd been hoping to eat for his lunch.

"Please help me, Deer!" he cried loudly. "Untangle the vines to set me free!"

Trembling, Deer shook her head.

"You'll eat me if I set you free."

"I promise I won't," said Tiger. "We can be friends."

Deer thought it would be better to have Tiger as a friend, rather than an enemy, so she untangled the vines.

But as soon as Tiger was free, he pounced on Deer.

"You promised not to eat me!" pleaded Deer.

"But I'm hungry!" roared Tiger.

Deer started to sob.

"What's going on?" asked Monkey, who was passing nearby. He'd heard Deer crying.

"Monkey," sniffed Deer, "do you think it is right for Tiger to eat me when I have just saved his life?"

"You did not save my life!" roared Tiger.

"Well, tigers do usually like to eat deer," replied Monkey. "Tiger, why don't you show me where you were, and then I can see if Deer really saved your life."

Grumbling to himself, Tiger let Deer tie the vines around his legs to show Monkey where he had been trapped.

Quick as a flash, Monkey jumped onto Deer's back.

"Come on, Deer," he chuckled. "Let's go!"

"Thanks, Monkey," said Deer. "Now you've saved *my* life!"

Tiger roared loudly as he found himself trapped once more.

Cats and Dogs

Hoddley, poddley, puddle, and fogs,
Cats are to marry the poodle dogs;
Cats in blue jackets and dogs in red hats,
What will become of the mice and the rats?

I Bought an Old Man

Hey diddle diddle,
And hey diddle dan!
And with a little money,
I bought an old man.
His legs were all crooked
And wrong ways set on,
So what do you think
Of my little old man?

Hearts

Hearts, like doors, will open with ease
To very, very little keys,
And don't forget that two of these
Are "I thank you" and "If you please."

New Hay

Willy boy, Willy boy,
Where are you going?
I will go with you,
If that I may.
I'm going to the meadow
To see them a-mowing,
I am going to help them
Turn the new hay.

Two Little Dogs

Two little dogs
Sat by the fire
Over a fender of coal-dust;
Said one little dog
To the other little dog,
If you don't talk—why, I must.

Mother Shuttle

Old Mother Shuttle
Lived in a coal-scuttle
Along with her dog and her cat;
What they ate I can't tell,
But 'tis known very well
That not one of the party was fat.

Rapunzel

Once upon a time, a poor young couple lived in a cottage next door to an old witch. The witch grew many vegetables in her garden, but she kept them all for herself.

One day, the couple had only a few potatoes left to eat.

"Surely it wouldn't matter if we took just a few vegetables," said the wife, gazing longingly over the wall.

So her husband quickly climbed into the garden and started to fill his basket. Suddenly he heard an angry voice.

"How dare you steal my vegetables?"

"Please don't hurt me," begged the young man. "My wife is going to have a baby soon, and she is hungry!"

"You may keep the vegetables," she croaked. "But you must give me the baby when it is born."

Terrified, the man had to agree.

Months later, his wife gave birth to a little girl. And although the parents begged and cried, the cruel witch took the baby. She called her Rapunzel.

Years passed, and Rapunzel grew up to be kind and beautiful. The witch was so afraid of losing her that she built a tall tower with no door and only one window. She planted thorn bushes all around it, then she locked Rapunzel in the tower.

Each day, Rapunzel brushed and combed her long golden locks. And each day, the witch came to visit her, standing at the foot of the tower and calling out, "Rapunzel, Rapunzel, let down your hair."

Rapunzel hung her hair out of the window and the witch climbed up it to sit and talk with her. But Rapunzel was very lonely. She sat at her window, and sang sadly.

One day, a prince rode by and heard the beautiful singing coming from the witch's garden. As he hid behind the wall, he saw the old witch call out, "Rapunzel, Rapunzel, let down your hair."

The prince saw a cascade of golden hair fall from the tower, and he watched the witch climb up it.

When the witch returned to her house, he crept to the tower. "Rapunzel, Rapunzel, let down your hair," he called softly.

Rapunzel let down her locks and the prince climbed up.

Rapunzel was very surprised to see the prince, and delighted when he said he wanted to be her friend. From then on, the prince came to visit her every day.

Months passed and Rapunzel and the prince fell in love.

"How can we be together?" Rapunzel cried. "The witch will never let me go."

So the prince brought some silk, which Rapunzel knotted together to make a ladder so that she could escape from the tower.

One day, without thinking, Rapunzel remarked to the witch, "It's much harder to pull you up than the prince!"

The witch was furious! "What prince?" she shouted.

She grabbed Rapunzel's long hair and cut it off. Then she used her magic to send Rapunzel far into the forest.

That evening, when the prince came to see Rapunzel, the witch held the golden hair out of the window and he climbed up into the tower, coming face to face with the old witch.

"You will never see Rapunzel again!" she screamed, and pushed the prince out of the window. He fell into the thorn bushes below. The sharp spikes scratched his eyes and blinded him. Weeping, he stumbled away.

After months of wandering, blind and lost, the prince heard beautiful, sad singing floating through the woods. He recognized Rapunzel's voice and called out to her.

"At last I have found you!" she cried. As her tears fell into the prince's eyes, his wounds healed, and he could see again.

Rapunzel had never been so happy. She and the prince were soon married, and they lived happily ever after, far away from the old witch and her empty tower.

Frère Jacques

Frère Jacques, Frère Jacques,
Dormez-vous, dormez-vous?
Sonnez les matines, sonnez les matines,
Ding, dang, dong! Ding, dang, dong!

O Lady Moon

O Lady Moon, your horns point toward the east:
Shine, be increased.
O Lady Moon, your horns point toward the west:
Wane, be at rest.

Ding, Dong, Bell

Ding, dong, bell,
Kitty's in the well!
Who put her in?
Little Johnny Flynn.
Who pulled her out?
Little Tommy Stout.
What a naughty boy was that
To try to drown poor pussycat,
Who never did any harm,
But killed the mice in his father's barn.

Muffin Man

Do you know the muffin man,
The muffin man, the muffin man,
Do you know the muffin man
Who lives in Drury Lane?

The Coachman

Up at Piccadilly, O!
The coachman takes his stand,
And when he meets a pretty girl,
He takes her by the hand;
Whip away for ever, O!
Drive away so clever, O!
All the way to Bristol, O!
He drives her four-in-hand.

The Miller of Dee

There was a jolly miller
Lived on the river Dee:
He worked and sang from morn till night,
No lark so blithe as he;
And this the burden of his song for ever used to be:
I jump me jerrime jee!
I care for nobody—no! not I,
Since nobody cares for me.

I Love My Mommy

One morning, Little Deer didn't want to play in his garden anymore.

"I want to see new things," he told his mommy.

"Then let's go exploring," said Mommy Deer.

"This way!" cried Little Deer, excitedly.

When Little Deer came to the stream, he slowly crossed the wobbly stones, watching the water as it trickled gently beside him.

"Don't get your feet wet," warned Mommy.

"I won't!" said Little Deer, as he wiggled and wobbled.

On the other side of the stream, Little Deer squeezed through the tangly bushes.

"Don't get stuck," warned Mommy.

"I won't! Hurry up, Mommy!" said Little Deer. "Look! A hill that goes up to the clouds!"

Little Deer climbed all the way to the top, panting with each step.

"I can see forever!" cried Little Deer, wobbling as he stood on tiptoes.

Then suddenly ...

"Wheeee!" cried Little Deer, as he slid down the other side of the hill into a meadow.

"Are you okay?" asked his mommy.

"Yes!" giggled Little Deer. "I am!"

Little Deer looked around the meadow. "Mommy?" he said anxiously. "Which way is home? I'm lost!"

"We'll soon find our way back," Mommy Deer said soothingly. "We just have to remember how we got here."

Little Deer thought and thought. At last, he began to remember....

"We came over the hill!" said Little Deer, and he scampered back up the hill. "I can see the way from here!"

Little Deer and his mommy skidded down the other side of the hill.

"We squeezed through those tangly bushes!" cried Little Deer, and they pushed through them.

"Which way now?" said Mommy Deer.

Little Deer heard the tinkling sound of a stream....

"The wobbly stones!" cheered Little Deer. "Don't get your feet wet, Mommy."

"I won't!" laughed Mommy Deer.

Little Deer knew the way from here. He ran as fast as he could, until he reached his garden.

"I love exploring," cried Little Deer happily. "And I love my mommy!"

Thank You

Thank you for your portrait,
I think it's very nice.
I've put it in the attic
To scare away the mice.

Utterly Cuckoo

Did you ever see a piglet all dressed up in polka dots,
Or a princess on her wedding day break out in bright green spots?
Did you ever see a colonel drinking coffee with a horse,
Or a three-legged mongoose? It's very rare, of course.
And if you've never seen a pink giraffe feeling blue,
Then you, my friend, are totally and utterly cuckoo!

Thirty White Horses on a Red Hill

Thirty white horses upon a red hill,
Now they tramp, now they champ,
Now they stand still.

The Foolish Wishes

There was once a poor woodcutter who was fed up of his hard life. One day, in the forest, a pixie suddenly appeared before him.

"You are a good man," said the pixie, "so I will grant you three wishes."

The woodcutter hurried home to tell his wife.

"We must think carefully before we make our wishes," said his wife.

"I agree," replied the woodcutter. "Let's celebrate our good fortune with a glass of freshly squeezed fruit juice. Oh, I wish we had some sausage to go with it."

No sooner had he said the words than a large sausage appeared on the table. The woodcutter's wife was furious and scolded her husband.

"Enough!" cried the woodcutter. "I wish the sausage was hanging from the end of your nose!"

And you can guess what happened.

The woodcutter had only one wish left.

"I could make myself a king," he sighed, "but my wife will never be happy with that sausage on her nose."

And so he wished the sausage would disappear. The couple did not become rich, but the woodcutter was glad to have his wife back to normal.

The Nightingale

A long, long time ago, Ancient China was ruled by a rich and proud emperor. The emperor loved to be surrounded by fine, expensive objects. The more they glittered with jewels and gold, the happier he was. He had a magnificent palace, filled with priceless treasures, which overlooked the most exquisite gardens.

Talk of the emperor's spectacular palace and gardens spread far and wide. Its beauty was held in such high esteem that many people wrote stories about it. The emperor liked to entertain himself by reading these books. He would sit in his throne room, nodding his approval at each new line of praise. He was a very happy man—until the day he read something that filled his proud heart with jealousy!

In the forest, beyond the emperor's gardens, there lived a tiny brown nightingale. The nightingale loved to sing. Every evening it would warble melodies so beautiful, they filled the heart with happiness.

The emperor hadn't even known of the nightingale's existence or the matchless beauty of its song until that moment.

"Get me the bird! I must hear it sing! How can anything be more beautiful than my palace?" screamed the emperor.

His lord-in-waiting hurried off to find the nightingale.

"Little bird, please come and sing for the emperor," he said.

"It would be an honor," chirped the tiny bird.

Back at the palace, the nightingale sang its glorious song. The tenderness of the melody touched the emperor's heart.

"You must stay and sing for me every day," he cried.

Day after day, the tiny bird sang his magnificent melodies for the emperor. He never complained about being kept in a cage, but he grew sad because he missed the freedom of his forest home.

Then, one day, the emperor received a gift. It was a clockwork nightingale made out of gold and jewels. Its song was beautiful, and the emperor loved his new toy so much that he lost interest in the real nightingale. The little nightingale escaped and flew back to his forest home.

A year went by, and the emperor played his mechanical bird day and night, until finally the toy broke. The emperor was devastated. Now he had no bird to sing to him. He was filled with sadness.

Day after day, he grew weaker and weaker. Then, one evening, as the emperor lay in his bed, close to death, a blissful harmony suddenly floated in through his open window. It was the nightingale.

"You came back," whispered the emperor. He felt comfort in his heart, and his fever disappeared. "I do not deserve your sweet music. How can I ever repay you?"

"I don't want anything," replied the nightingale. "Knowing that I have touched your heart is enough. I can't come and live in your palace, but I will visit you every evening."

The emperor's face filled with happiness. He realized how foolish and empty his love of riches was. He had been given a second chance, and he vowed to rule his empire wisely from then on.

As Quiet As a ...

Tabitha mouse was trying to sleep. But every time she
closed her eyes, she heard, "CAW! CAW!" It was very
loud, and it was keeping her awake. She sat up and peeped out
of her window. There were seven crows sitting in a row on a
telephone line. She opened her window and leaned out.

"Excuse me, crows," she said. "Could you be a bit quieter?
I'm trying to sleep." But the crows just stared at her and said,
"CAW" even more loudly.

"Oh dear," said Tabitha, wondering how she could get them
to understand. She put one of her tiny fingers up to her mouth
and said, "Shhh! As quiet as a whisper."

The crows hunched up their shoulders and tried their best. "CSHHHHAW! CSHHHHAW!" Tabitha put her paws over her ears. It was even louder than before! She thought again, then smiled. Tapping her head, she said, "As quiet as a thought."

The crows looked at each other and shrugged. They didn't know what she meant. They all started to caw more loudly than ever, wondering what the little mouse was saying.

"No, no," said Tabitha with a sigh.

Just then, she had an idea. She scurried outside and stood on the sidewalk underneath the crows. She waited for them to see her, then she raised her hands to signal for them to pay attention. When they were all watching, she rose up on her tiptoes and ran up and down in front of them. Suddenly, the crows understood. Tabitha was being "as quiet as a mouse"!

The crows shut their beaks and didn't say another word. Tabitha went back to her room, took off her robe, and crept into bed. She peeped through the curtains at the crows, who had tucked their heads under their wings.

"Goodnight," said Tabitha, and she lay down and fell fast asleep.

Fishes Swim

Fishes swim in water clear,
Birds fly up into the air,
Serpents creep along the ground,
Boys and girls run round and round.

Feathers

Cackle, cackle, Mother Goose,
Have you any feathers loose?
Truly have I, pretty fellow,
Half enough to fill a pillow.
Here are quills, take one or two,
And down to make a bed for you.

Three Blind Mice

Three blind mice, three blind mice!
See how they run, see how they run!
They all ran after the farmer's wife,
Who cut off their tails with a carving knife,
Did ever you see such a thing in your life,
As three blind mice?

Robin and Pussycat

Little Robin Redbreast jumped upon a wall,
Pussycat jumped after him,
And almost got a fall!
Little Robin chirped and sang,
And what did Pussycat say?
Pussycat said, "Mew,"
And Robin jumped away.

Pussycat and Robin

Little Robin Redbreast sat upon a tree,
Up went Pussycat, and down went he!
Down came Pussycat, and away Robin ran;
Says little Robin Redbreast,
"Catch me if you can!"

Cut Thistles

Cut thistles in May,
They'll grow in a day;
Cut them in June,
That is too soon;
Cut them in July,
Then they will die.

Help from Huggle Buggle

Get set, Huggle Buggle,
Let's all play outside.
We'll run and we'll jump,
We'll swing and we'll slide.

Come on, Huggle Buggle,
Let's get dressed and go!
I'll wear my red sweater—
Where is it? Oh no!

I must find my sweater
Before I can play.
It was in the drawer—
Someone took it away!

Lost! Gone!
Where could it be?
I wish Huggle Buggle
Could find it for me.

What a surprise!
It's my friend Ellie Nellie.
My sweater's an apron
Tied up around her belly!

Thanks, Huggle Buggle!
You're the best-ever bear.
But I'm still not quite ready—
What else should I wear?

What if the wind
Blows the leaves on the ground?
I could wrap up tight
Before running around.

I'll pull on my gloves,
My snuggly hat, too....
But where is my scarf?
Oh, what should I do?

It must be here somewhere—
It's my red and white one!
I saw it just yesterday—
Where has it gone?

Lost! Vanished!
Where could it be?
I wish Huggle Buggle
Could find it for me.

My scarf is a jump rope—
That's very funny!
But who is holding it?
Babbity Bunny!

Okay, Huggle Buggle,
What now? Do you know?
If everyone's ready,
It's playtime—LET'S GO!

Verity's Fairy Tale

Verity's family lived in a castle. Verity loved living there, as her favorite books were all about handsome princes and beautiful princesses.

Verity even hoped that, one day, a prince would visit her castle and they would have an amazing adventure together, just like in her fairy-tale books. If only her prince would hurry up!

One day, Verity was peering out of the window in the highest tower, when she heard a rumbling noise.

"The steps!" she cried. "They're collapsing!"

The winding staircase fell away, and Verity was stuck.

"How will I get down now?" she thought.

Verity looked out of the window again, but not a single prince was galloping to her rescue on a white horse. All she could see was her little brother playing in the garden.

"There's only one thing to do," Verity said. "I'll have to rescue myself."

Thinking quickly, Verity made a ladder out of some ivy vines that were clinging to the wall outside. Then she attached them to a hook inside the tower, and climbed down through the space where the steps used to be.

Down, down, down she went, and her ivy ladder spun and swung, but she hung on tight.

At last, Verity reached the bottom of the tower.

"I did it!" she cheered. "I rescued myself!"

And from that day on, Verity stopped waiting to have an adventure with a handsome prince ... Instead, she went ahead and had them all on her own!

See a Pin and Pick It Up

See a pin and pick it up,
All the day you'll have good luck;
See a pin and let it lay,
Bad luck you'll have all the day!

Miss Mary Mack

Miss Mary Mack, Mack, Mack,
All dressed in black, black, black,
With silver buttons, buttons, buttons,
All down her back, back, back.
She went upstairs to make her bed,
She made a mistake and bumped her head;
She went downstairs to wash the dishes,
She made a mistake and washed her wishes;
She went outside to hang her clothes,
She made a mistake and hung her nose.

Ring Around the Rosy

Ring around the rosy,
A pocket full of posies,
Ashes! Ashes!
We all fall down!

Mr. Nobody

Mr. Nobody is a nice young man,
He comes to the door with his hat in his hand.
Down she comes, all dressed in silk,
A rose in her bosom, as white as milk.
She takes off her gloves, she shows me her ring,
Tomorrow, tomorrow, the wedding begins.

Little Sally Waters

Little Sally Waters,
Sitting in the sun,
Crying and weeping,
For a young man.
Rise, Sally, rise,
Dry your weeping eyes,
Fly to the east,
Fly to the west,
Fly to the one you love the best.

Georgie Porgie

Georgie Porgie, pudding and pie,
Kissed the girls and made them cry;
When the boys came out to play,
Georgie Porgie ran away.

The Story of the Blue Jackal

Once upon a time, there lived a jackal named Chandarava. One day, he was very hungry. He couldn't find any food in the jungle, so he wandered into a nearby village to search for something to eat.

The dogs in the village saw him and started to chase him. Trying to escape, Chandarava ran into a house. It belonged to a washerwoman. Inside was a big vat of blue dye. Without thinking, Chandarava jumped into the vat to hide. His entire body was dyed blue. When he climbed out, he no longer looked like a jackal.

The dogs were confused. They had never seen a blue animal before. Terrified, they ran away.

Hungry and fed up, Chandarava returned to the jungle. The blue dye wouldn't wash off! When the other animals saw him, they were frightened and ran away. Chandarava didn't want to be alone, so he came up with a clever plan.

"Don't be afraid," said the blue creature. "The Lord of Creations has sent me here to be your king and to protect you. Come and live in peace in my kingdom."

The other animals were convinced by Chandarava's words.

"O, Master, we await your commands. Please let us know whatever you want," they said.

The blue jackal gave everyone jobs—mostly to serve him! He enjoyed being treated like royalty, but he was also a kind and fair ruler, and the animals lived peacefully together.

One evening, after enjoying a particularly fine feast, Chandarava heard a pack of jackals howling in the distance.

Unable to hide his natural instinct, Chandarava howled back. When the other animals heard this, they realized that Chandarava was only a jackal and not the king he was pretending to be.

Chandarava knew he had been wrong to fool the animals. He tried to explain why he had lied, but it was too late. The animals were so angry that they chased him out of the jungle.

So the blue jackal ended up spending the rest of his days alone after all.

Come to Bed, Says Sleepyhead

"Come to bed," says Sleepyhead,
"Let's stay a while," says Slow,
"Put on the pot," says Greedy-gut,
"Let's sup before we go."

Wee Willie Winkie

Wee Willie Winkie
Runs through the town,
Upstairs and downstairs
In his nightgown.
Rapping at the window,
Crying through the lock,
"Are the children all in bed?
It's past eight o'clock."

Brahms' Lullaby

Lullaby, and good night,
With rosy bed light,
With lilies overspread,
Is my sweet baby's head.
Lullaby, and good night,
You're your mother's delight,
Shining angels beside
My darling abide.

Go to Sleep

Go to sleep, my baby,
Close your pretty eyes,
Angels are above us,
Peeping through the skies.
Great big moon is shining,
Stars begin to peep.
Time for little babies
All to go to sleep.

Diddle, Diddle, Dumpling

Diddle, diddle, dumpling, my son John,
Went to bed with his trousers on.
One shoe off, and the other shoe on,
Diddle, diddle, dumpling, my son John.

My Best Friend

Emily was playing in the backyard with her favorite doll, Hannah.

"Hello, Emily!" called a cheerful voice.

It was Sarah, who lived next door. The two girls were best friends.

"Can I play with Hannah, too?" asked Sarah, reaching out to pick her up.

Emily held on tightly to Hannah. She was a very special doll, and Emily didn't like anybody else playing with her.

"Hannah's tired," said Emily. "I think I'll put her to bed. Then I'll come back and play with you."

For the rest of the morning, Emily and Sarah played in Emily's treehouse. It was their special hideout, and nobody else was allowed in it.

They both thought it was great living next door to one another.

The next day, both girls got up early and ran down to the front yard. They were very excited. They were going on vacation together. Every year, they went to the same vacation cottage. Sarah was traveling with Emily's family. That way, they could talk to each other on the journey.

"Can Hannah sit between us?" Sarah asked Emily, as they climbed into the car.

"Sorry," said Emily. "Hannah says she wants to sit by the window." And she tucked Hannah safely out of Sarah's reach.

At last they arrived at the cottage, and the girls raced from room to room, checking that nothing had changed since last year.

At bedtime, they snuggled down in their cozy beds in the attic. They loved sharing a room on vacation. They stayed awake long after the lights went out, talking and laughing together.

This vacation was the best one yet. One day, Sarah rode her bicycle without training wheels for the first time. The next day, Emily did too. Soon, the girls were racing each other.

"Can we keep racing each other when we get home?" Sarah asked her mom and dad. Her mom frowned.

"Hmmm," she began. "There's something we've been meaning to tell you. We're moving away. Daddy's got a new job, and we've found a wonderful new house."

Emily and Sarah couldn't believe their ears. They wouldn't be neighbors anymore!

"It's not too far. You'll still be able to see Emily on weekends and during vacations," Dad said.

"But I don't want to move!" cried Sarah. She threw her arms around Emily. "You won't forget me, will you?" she whispered.

Back at home, after the vacation, the last days of summer flew by. On the morning that Sarah and her family were due to leave, Emily and her parents came outside to say goodbye.

"I've brought you a present to remember me by," said Sarah, handing Emily a gift. Emily ripped off the paper.

Nestled inside was a gorgeous golden heart necklace.

"It's beautiful!" Emily smiled. Then she rushed inside her house. She came out a minute later carrying Hannah.

"Here," she said, putting the doll into Sarah's arms. "Hannah will keep you company until you make friends at your new house."

Sarah was speechless. She gave Emily an enormous hug.

Emily grinned. "Sharing really is great," she declared. "Especially sharing things with your very best friend."

Here Comes a Widow

Here comes a widow from Barbary-land,
With all her children in her hand;
One can brew, and one can bake,
And one can make a wedding cake.
Pray take one, pray take two,
Pray take one that pleases you.

Little Husband

I had a little husband,
No bigger than my thumb;
I put him in a pint pot,
And there I bade him drum.
I gave him some garters
To garter up his hose,
And a little silk handkerchief
To wipe his pretty nose.

Rock-a-bye, Baby

Rock-a-bye, baby, thy cradle is green;
Father's a nobleman, Mother's a queen,
And Betty's a lady and wears a gold ring,
And Johnny's a drummer and drums for the king.

Our Baby

Goodness, our baby makes a lot of noise!
He bangs his crib and throws out all his toys.
But there's one time I love to take a peep,
And that's when, finally, he falls asleep.

Clap Hands

Clap hands, Daddy's coming up the wagon way,
His pockets full of money, and his hands full of clay.

Dance to Your Daddy

Dance to your daddy,
My little babby;
Dance to your daddy,
My little lamb.

You shall have a fishy,
In a little dishy;
You shall have a fishy
When the boat comes in.

Balloon Adventure

Freddie had always wondered what it would be like to fly like a bird. One evening, he talked to his dad about it.

"Oh, it would be amazing!" said Dad. "Looking down on the world, soaring through the clouds.... I know, why don't we organize a balloon ride, then we can see for ourselves!"

"That would be awesome, Dad!" cried Freddie, excitedly. "We'll be able to see everything from a bird's-eye view."

So a few days later, on a warm, breezy evening, Freddie and his dad set off on their balloon adventure.

They settled into the big wicker basket, and then they were off … floating higher and higher. Up, up, and away in the big pink balloon!

Freddie couldn't believe his eyes....

Up above, he could see planes soaring through the clouds.

"I wonder where they are going?" he sighed, as he watched their fluffy vapor trails fade into the distant sun-tinted skies.

"Look over there, Freddie," cried Dad, pointing at a flock of birds.

They soared past, flying in a V formation.

As the breeze rustled through his hair, Freddie glanced down. Everything looked tiny! Houses and trees appeared in miniature, like models. The cars crawled along winding ribbons of roads like marching ants.

Dad grinned at Freddie. "How are you enjoying your ride?" he asked.

"It's so cool," laughed Freddie. "I feel like I'm a bird, too. I can't believe we are so high in the air!"

The balloon drifted along silently and over the crest of a hill. Suddenly, the sky was filled with other balloons of all shapes and sizes. Freddie could see a smiling elephant and an inflated bear with a sleepy face. Hovering nearby was a shimmering butterfly and a funny bunny balloon.

"A balloon carnival!" cried Dad, smiling and waving as they floated along on the breeze with the other balloons.

Freddie glanced off into the distance. He could see the silhouette of a city, and the sun was beginning to dip toward the horizon. It was time to head home.

Slowly, the balloon glided lower and lower, down and down ... until it landed with a gentle bump on the ground.

Freddie hugged his dad.

"Thanks, Dad," he said. "This has been the best day EVER!"

Dad smiled. "Let's go on another balloon adventure soon."

Twinkle, Twinkle

Twinkle, twinkle, little star,
How I wonder what you are!
Up above the world so high,
Like a diamond in the sky.

When the blazing sun is gone,
When he nothing shines upon,
Then you show your little light,
Twinkle, twinkle, all the night.

Then the traveler in the dark,
Thanks you for your tiny spark,
He could not see which way to go,
If you did not twinkle so.

As your bright and tiny spark,
Lights the traveler in the dark—
Though I know not what you are,
Twinkle, twinkle, little star.

Sleep, Baby, Sleep

Sleep, baby, sleep,
Your father keeps the sheep;
Your mother shakes the dreamland tree
And from it fall sweet dreams for thee;
Sleep, baby, sleep.

Sleep, baby, sleep,
The large stars are the sheep;
The little stars are the lambs, I guess,
And the gentle moon is the shepherdess;
Sleep, baby, sleep.

Sleep, baby, sleep,
Your father keeps the sheep;
Your mother guards the lambs this night,
And keeps them safe till morning light;
Sleep, baby, sleep.

Goodnight, Little One

It had been a busy day on Blue Lake Farm. When the sun set and the moon came out, all the animals were ready for their beds. The stars twinkled, and everyone closed their eyes and fell asleep. Everyone, that is, except for Molly's kittens.

Molly had five kittens named Squeaker, Crumble, Ginger, Biscuit, and Titch. Each one of them was full to the brim with mischief and fun.

"It's time for bed," said Molly. "Come into the barn and snuggle up on the hay."

But the kittens started leaping between the hay bales to see who could jump the farthest. They tumbled and giggled and jumped. They meowed and bounced and hid. The one thing they didn't do was snuggle up and go to sleep.

Suddenly, Molly had an idea.

"All right," she said. "You can stay up all night long and play as much as you like, on one condition. You are not allowed to fall asleep! No yawning or rubbing your eyes. No catnapping in the corner. Stay awake and play to your hearts' content."

"Hurray!" cheered the kittens. Molly sat in the doorway of the barn to watch them. Squeaker and Biscuit darted into the grass outside the barn and started jumping on each other.

"We're frogs!" Squeaker panted. "Boing! Boing! No one can jump higher than me!"

Crumble and Ginger leaped onto the farm fence and ran up and down like tightrope walkers, springing over each other and keeping their balance perfectly.

Titch scrambled onto the farm roof and sat beside the weathervane, meowing at the moon in his loudest outside voice. Molly put her paws over her ears and hoped that the farmer wouldn't wake up.

Next, all five kittens raced over to the farm's small pond. They played chase, running in circles around the water until they were all so dizzy that they couldn't walk straight. Crumble suddenly gave a big yawn.

"No yawning!" Molly called to him. "You must stay awake."

The kittens ran back over to the barn, but Molly noticed that they weren't quite as bouncy or as loud as they had been before.

"I'm just going to have a little sit down for a minute," said Crumble. He leaned against Molly, and his eyes closed. Molly gave a smile.

The other four kittens started to chase some mice. The mice ran through the pigsty, around the chicken coop, through the cow shed, and into the meadows. On the way back to the barn, Biscuit and Squeaker kept stopping to sit down and rub their heavy eyes.

"We're just going to sit with you for a minute to warm up," they told Molly. Their eyelids drooped, and Molly's smile grew a little wider.

Some birds were swooping around the farmyard. Squeaker started to jump up, trying to knock them out of the air with his paw. But the birds were too quick for him, and soon Squeaker walked over to Molly, panting.

"I'm just going to get my breath back," he said, lying down next to Crumble. He was asleep as soon as he had stopped speaking.

Titch was trying to pounce on his shadow.

"I'm not going to sleep like the others," he said.

Molly smiled at him.

"I love you, Titch."

Titch smiled back, and ran over to give Molly a big cuddle.

"I love you, too," he said. When Molly looked down, she saw that Titch had fallen fast asleep in the middle of the cuddle.

Molly wrapped her tail around all five kittens to keep them safe and warm. Then she closed her eyes and drifted off to sleep in the light of the moon.

Mother Hulda

There was once a woman with two daughters. Her stepdaughter was hard-working, while her own daughter was lazy. The woman preferred her birth daughter, and made her stepdaughter do all the work around the house.

One day, the woman gave her stepdaughter an enormous basket of wool.

"Take this wool and spin it all. Don't come back until it's finished," she told her stepdaughter.

So the stepdaughter sat and span until her fingers bled. Just as she lowered a bucket into the well, ready to scoop up some water to wash her fingers, she accidentally dropped the spindle. It fell into the water at the bottom of the well with a PLOP!

The girl climbed down to find the spindle, and, at the bottom of the well, she found herself in a strange land with orange trees, blue grass, and a pink sky.

After a while, she reached a little house. A kind woman named Mother Hulda lived there. She gave the girl food and shelter. In return, the girl helped Mother Hulda with all her chores.

Even though Mother Hulda was kinder than her stepmother, the girl began to feel homesick.

"I would like to return home," said the girl.

So Mother Hulda gave the girl back her spindle, and, as the girl left the strange land, a shower of gold coins fell at her feet.

When the girl arrived home with the coins, her stepmother was amazed. She wanted the same thing to happen to her own lazy daughter.

"Do just as your sister did," she told the idle girl.

But the stepmother's daughter could not be bothered to sit and spin, so she stuck her hands into a thorny bush to make them bleed. Then she dropped the spindle down the well and climbed in after it.

The girl knocked on Mother Hulda's door, asking for food and shelter. After eating, she fell asleep, snoring like a pig!

"Give me back my spindle. I want to go home now," said the rude girl to Mother Hulda when she woke up.

So Mother Hulda took the girl back to the bottom of the well. But instead of gold coins, it was tar that fell at her feet.

The girl returned to her mother, who tried to scrub her shoes clean. But the tar was stuck fast, and has remained there ever since.

Hickory, Dickory, Dock

Hickory, dickory, dock,
The mouse ran up the clock.
The clock struck one,
The mouse ran down,
Hickory, dickory, dock.

Bat, Bat

Bat, bat, come under my hat,
And I'll give you a slice of bacon,
And when I bake I'll give you a cake,
If I am not mistaken.

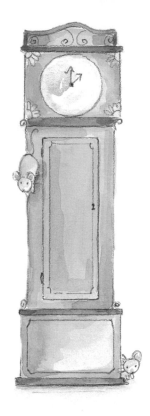

Itsby Bitsy Spider

Itsby Bitsy spider
Climbed up the water spout;
Down came the rain
And washed the spider out.
Out came the sun
And dried up all the rain;
And the Itsby Bitsy spider
Climbed up the spout again.

Little Jack Horner

Little Jack Horner,
Sat in a corner,
Eating a Christmas pie.
He put in his thumb,
And pulled out a plum,
And said, "What a good boy am I!"

Bow, Wow, Wow

Bow, wow, wow,
Whose dog art thou?
"Little Tom Tinker's dog,
Bow, wow, wow."

The Cold Old House

I know a house, and a cold old house,
A cold old house by the sea.
If I were a mouse in that cold old house
What a cold, cold mouse I'd be!

The Lost Shark

Thalia the clownfish and her friends were always being chased by sharks. One day, Thalia saw a baby shark on its own. None of Thalia's friends would help him.

"We don't like sharks," they said.

Thalia felt sorry for the baby. He looked so sad.

Trembling, she whispered, "Are you all right?"

"I've lost my mommy," the baby shark cried.

Thalia had never seen a baby with so many sharp teeth. But she imagined how scared he must feel.

"Come on," she said. "I'll help you find her."

Before long, they found the mommy shark. She had been swimming around, looking for her little one.

"Oh, you've found him," she said to Thalia. Then she bared her teeth ... and smiled. Then added, "Thank you!"

Thalia and the baby shark made friends, and Thalia soon found out that the sharks had only been chasing the fish to play.

"Sharks aren't so bad after all!" Thalia said.

Granny's Garden

One day, when Megan visited her granny, no one answered the door. Feeling curious, Megan walked around the side of the house and into the garden. On the grass, she saw half a pumpkin, a spindle, a glass slipper, and a mermaid comb. There was even a pot of gold with a rainbow bursting out of it.

"That's odd!" thought Megan. "I've not seen these here before."

Then, all of a sudden, Granny flew across the sky, holding a wand and wearing wings. Megan's mouth fell open.

"You're a fairy godmother!" Megan gasped.

"I'm *the* fairy godmother," said Granny. "I've just come back from visiting Cinderella, and now I have to dash out for tea with my fairy friends. Next time you visit, I'll tell you all about it. But for now, promise to keep my secret?"

"Of course!" gasped Megan.

Then Granny waved her wand and disappeared in a swirl of sparkles.

Megan couldn't wait for her next trip to Granny's house!

The Gnome

Once upon a time, there was a king who had a special
apple tree in his palace garden. The fruit was delicious,
but the tree was cursed. The king forbade anyone, including his
own three daughters, to eat the apples: if they did, they would
find themselves at the bottom of a deep well.

Of course, his daughters couldn't resist the sweet fruits, and
they each ate an apple.

In a flash, the three girls disappeared deep underground.
When they didn't return home that evening, the king was
distraught. He put out a proclamation saying he would offer a
huge reward for their safe return.

Three young huntsmen, who were also brothers, set out to look for the princesses. They had been traveling for a few days when they came across a cottage in the forest. There was no sign of anyone living there, and as the two elder brothers didn't like their youngest brother, Hans, they told him to stay at the cottage in case anyone came home. Then they went out to look for the princesses, hoping to get the reward for themselves.

The brothers hadn't been gone long when a strange little gnome appeared in front of Hans. He told the younger brother where the princesses were hidden and how to rescue them.

"The princesses are at the bottom of a deep well in the middle of this forest," explained the gnome. "But go alone because your brothers will betray you."

Hans did as he was told, and he soon found the princesses. They were very happy to see him.

That evening, when Hans' brothers returned to the cottage, they were furious to see that Hans had found the princesses himself. So they told Hans to go home, then they took the princesses back to the palace, where they told the king that *they* had rescued the princesses. But the princesses wanted to thank Hans—their real rescuer—so they told their father the truth.

As punishment, the king banished the two elder brothers from his kingdom for good. Then he rewarded Hans with a huge pot of gold.

And, just to be safe, the king had the apple tree cut down!

Baa, Baa, Black Sheep

Baa, baa, black sheep, have you any wool?
Yes, sir, yes, sir, three bags full;
One for the master, one for the dame,
And one for the little boy who lives down the lane.

A Thorn

I went to the wood and got it;
I sat me down and looked at it;
The more I looked at it the less I liked it;
And I brought it home because I couldn't help it.

Cross Patch

Cross patch,
Draw the latch,
Sit by the fire and spin;
Take a cup,
And drink it up,
Then call your neighbors in.

I Love Little Pussycat

I love little pussycat, her coat is so warm;
And if I don't hurt her she'll do me no harm.
So I'll not pull her tail nor drive her away,
But pussycat and I very gently will play.

Pussycat Mole

Pussycat Mole,
Jumped over a coal,
And in her best petticoat
Burned a great hole.
Poor pussycat's weeping,
She'll have no more milk,
Until her best petticoat's
Mended with silk.

On the Grassy Banks

On the grassy banks
Lambkins at their pranks;
Woolly sisters, woolly brothers,
Jumping off their feet,
While their woolly mothers
Watch them and bleat.

Snow White

Once there was a queen who longed for a daughter. As she sat sewing by her window one winter's day, she pricked her finger on the needle. As blood fell from her finger she thought, "I wish I had a daughter with lips as red as blood, hair as black as ebony wood, and skin as white as the snow outside!"

Before long, the queen gave birth to a baby girl with blood-red lips, ebony hair, and skin as white as snow. She called her Snow White.

Sadly, the queen died, and the king married again. His new wife was beautiful, but vain.

She had a magic mirror, and every day, she looked into it and asked:

"Mirror, mirror, on the wall,
Who is the fairest of them all?"

And every day, the mirror replied:

"You, O Queen, are the fairest of them all."

But Snow White became more and more beautiful every day.

One morning, when the queen asked the mirror who was the fairest, the mirror replied:

"You, O Queen, are fair, it's true.

But young Snow White is fairer than you."

Furious, the queen told her huntsman, "Take Snow White into the forest and kill her!"

The huntsman led Snow White deep into the forest, but could not bear to hurt her.

"Run far away from here," he said.

As darkness fell, Snow White came upon a little cottage. She knocked softly on the door, but there was no answer, so she let herself in.

Inside, Snow White found a table and seven tiny chairs.

Upstairs, there were seven little beds.

Snow White lay down on the seventh bed and fell fast asleep.

She awoke to find seven little men staring at her in amazement.

"Who are you?" she asked.

"We are the seven dwarves who live here," said one dwarf. "Who are you?"

"I am Snow White," she replied, and she told them her sad story.

"You can stay with us," said the eldest dwarf kindly.

Every day, the seven dwarves went to work while Snow White cooked and cleaned the cottage.

"Don't open the door to anyone," they told her, worried the wicked queen might find her.

Meanwhile, when the wicked queen asked her mirror once more who was the fairest that day, it replied:

"You, O Queen, are fair, it's true,
But Snow White is still fairer than you.
Deep in the forest with seven little men
Snow White is living in a cozy den."

The queen was furious and vowed to kill Snow White herself. So she added poison to a juicy apple, then set off to the forest, disguised as a peddler woman.

"Try my juicy apples!" she called out, knocking on the door of the seven dwarves' cottage.

Snow White remembered the dwarves' warning, so she just opened the window to take a look.

When the queen offered Snow White an apple, she took a big bite. The poisoned piece got stuck in her throat, and she fell to the ground.

When the seven dwarves returned, they were heartbroken to find their beloved Snow White dead. They couldn't bear to bury her, so they put her in a glass coffin and placed it in the forest, where they took turns watching over her.

One day, a prince rode by and saw Snow White. The dwarves told him her sad story.

"Please let me take her away," begged the prince. The dwarves could see he loved Snow White, and they agreed to let her go.

As the prince's servants lifted the coffin, one of them stumbled, jolting the poisoned apple from Snow White's throat, and she came back to life.

When Snow White saw the handsome prince, she fell deeply in love with him.

They soon married, and lived happily ever after, together with the dwarves.

Anna Maria

Anna Maria, she sat on the fire;
The fire was too hot, she sat on the pot;
The pot was too round, she sat on the ground;
The ground was too flat, she sat on the cat;
The cat ran away with Maria on her back.

Round-eared Cap

A pretty little girl in a round-eared cap
I met in the streets the other day;
She gave me such a thump,
That my heart it went bump;
I thought I should have fainted away!
I thought I should have fainted away!

Goldy Locks, Goldy Locks

Goldy locks, goldy locks,
Wilt thou be mine?
Thou shall not wash dishes,
Nor yet feed the swine;

But sit on a cushion,
And sew a fine seam,
And feed upon strawberries,
Sugar, and cream.

There Was a Little Girl

There was a little girl, and she had a little curl
Right in the middle of her forehead;
When she was good she was very, very good,
But when she was bad she was horrid.

Little Miss Muffet

Little Miss Muffet
Sat on a tuffet,
Eating her curds and whey;
Along came a spider,
Who sat down beside her,
And frightened Miss Muffet away.

The Stone Soup

Samuel was on his way to visit a friend, but he was cold, tired, and hungry. Up ahead, he saw a little cottage.

"Please could you spare me some food?" he asked the owner of the cottage.

"I don't have any," lied the old woman.

"Could I borrow your pot and cook some tasty soup?" Samuel asked.

"You may, if you share it with me," replied the old woman.

So Samuel filled the pot with water. Then he found two large stones outside. He cleaned them and put them in the pot.

"What kind of soup are you making?" asked the old woman in surprise.

"Stone soup," replied Samuel. "It's wonderful, but it would taste even better with some vegetables."

"I've got carrots and potatoes," the old woman said.

Samuel added the vegetables and stirred the soup.

Then he said, "With seasoning, it would be perfect!"

"I've got salt and pepper," replied the old woman.

Soon the soup was ready. "Hmm, delicious," said the old woman, not realizing she was sharing her food after all!

Ice Cream

Ice cream, ice cream, a penny a lump!
The more you eat, the more you jump.

Christmas Eve

On Christmas Eve I turned the spit,
I burned my fingers, I feel it yet;
The little cock sparrow flew over the table,
The pot began to play with the ladle.

Gingerbread Men

Smiling girls, rosy boys,
Come and buy my little toys:
Monkeys made of gingerbread,
And sugar horses painted red.

The Golden Goose

There was once a man who had three sons. Two of them were clever, but everyone thought the youngest, named Peter, was silly.

One day, the father sent the eldest son, Luke, into the forest to chop down a tree. He was just about to start work when a little old man appeared.

"Please can I have some food?" the old man asked.

"If I give some to you, there won't be much for me," Luke replied. Then he began to chop down the tree.

As if by magic, the eldest son's ax slipped and he cut his arm, so he had to go home.

As the wood still needed chopping, the father sent the middle son, Paul, into the forest. Once again, the little old man appeared.

"Please can I have some food?" asked the old man.

But the middle son refused. "I won't have much left if I give some to you," he replied.

Suddenly, Paul's ax slipped and he cut his leg. So he had to go home, too.

"Father, let me chop down the tree," said Peter.

His father laughed. "What makes you think you can do it if your brothers can't?"

But Peter begged his father until he gave in.

Peter set off to the forest. It wasn't long before he met the little old man.

"Please can I have some food?" asked the old man.

"There's not much," Peter said. "But you are welcome to share it with me."

"You're a kind boy," said the old man, as they sat down to eat. "Let me give you something in return."

The old man told Peter to cut down the tree and see what was inside its roots.

Peter did as the old man said. Inside the roots was a goose with golden feathers. Puzzled, Peter looked around for the old man, but he had mysteriously disappeared.

By now it was getting late, so Peter picked up the goose and went to find an inn for the night.

The innkeeper had three daughters, and they were fascinated by the goose's golden feathers. One by one, they reached out to pluck a golden feather, but the moment they touched the bird, they stuck to the goose and couldn't let go!

In the morning, the girls were still stuck to the goose. So Peter set out for home, with the three girls trailing behind him.

When other people saw the strange procession, they tried to pull the girls free, only to become stuck too!

Peter's journey took him through a city ruled by a king. The king's daughter was so sad and the king couldn't make her happy. In desperation, he offered her hand in marriage to anyone who could make her laugh.

As soon as the princess saw Peter's ridiculous procession, she began to laugh as if she would never stop.

The king was thrilled. "You may marry my daughter!" he told Peter.

So Peter and the princess soon married. They lived a happy life, full of laughter, and no one made fun of Peter anymore.

The Enchanted Garden

Princess Sylvie loved to walk through the meadows to look at the flowers.

One day, she found an overgrown path in her favorite meadow. She asked a woman where the path led.

"To the garden of the enchantress!" said the woman. "You can go and look, but they say that whatever you do, don't pick the flowers."

Princess Sylvie followed the path until she came to a cottage with the prettiest garden she had ever seen, filled with flowers of every color and perfume.

Princess Sylvie went back to the garden every day. Soon she forgot all about the enchantress, and one day, she picked a rose from the garden and took it back to the castle. As she put it in water, Princess Sylvie suddenly remembered the warning!

But months passed and nothing happened. The rose stayed as fresh as the day it was picked. Forgetting her fears, Princess Sylvie went back to the enchanted garden.

But when she saw the garden, Princess Sylvie wanted to cry. The grass was brown. All the flowers had withered.

Then she heard someone weeping. Inside the cottage, the enchantress was sitting by the fire, crying. She was old and bent. Princess Sylvie was afraid, but she felt sorry for her.

"What happened to your lovely garden?" Princess Sylvie asked.

"Someone picked a rose from it!" said the enchantress. "The garden is under a spell. The picked flower will live forever, but the rest of the flowers must die! And when the rose was picked, my magic was lost, too, and I too am beginning to wither and die!"

"What can I do?" said Princess Sylvie.

"Only a princess can help," the enchantress replied. "She must bring me six sacks of stinging nettles! And no princess would do that!"

Princess Sylvie gathered six sacks of nettles, not caring that they stung her, and took them back to the enchantress.

The enchantress said, "But the nettles must be picked by a princess."

"I am a princess," said Princess Sylvie.

The enchantress made a magic potion with the nettles and drank it. Instantly, the garden became beautiful again. Princess Sylvie gasped! Gone was the bent old lady. In her place was a beautiful young woman.

"My garden is restored," smiled the enchantress, "and so am I!"

And so the enchantress and the princess became great friends and shared the enchanted garden.

The Penny Wise Monkey

Once upon a time, there lived a king who ruled over a rich and prosperous kingdom. But the king was never happy with what he had. He always wanted more.

One day, he set out with his men on yet another mission to take over yet another kingdom. They trekked through the forest all day. By the evening, they were exhausted and stopped to take some rest.

After supper, the soldiers fed their horses apples. In a nearby tree, a hungry monkey watched them. Some of the apples fell on the ground. The monkey jumped down from the tree, grabbed a handful of them, and scampered back up to the top.

As he sat enjoying the apples, one slipped from his hand and fell to the ground. Without thinking, the greedy monkey dropped all the other apples in his hands and ran down to look for the lost apple. He couldn't find it, and climbed back up the tree, empty-handed. His greed made him lose all that he had.

The king, who had been watching the monkey closely, realized that his own need to have more and more might also leave him with nothing one day.

"I will not be like this foolish monkey, who lost so much to gain so little!" he cried. "I will go back to my own kingdom and enjoy what I have."

The Monkeys and the Moon

A long, long time ago, a band of monkeys lived in a forest. In the middle of the forest there was a deep well.

One night, when the leader of the monkeys went to the well to get a drink, he saw the reflection of the moon in the water.

"Oh no!" he gasped. "The moon has fallen in the water. Our sky will have no moon. We must get it out!"

The other monkeys agreed. They formed a chain, each holding onto the tail of the one before them, while the monkey at the top of the chain held on to a branch to support them all.

The branch began to bend under the weight of all the monkeys. Suddenly ... CRACK! The branch broke and the monkeys tumbled into the well. The water rippled as they all scrambled to get out of the well, and the reflection of the moon disappeared.

Up above the forest, the moon shone its silvery light on the silly, wet monkeys!

The Big Freeze

It had been snowing all day, but when evening came, the flakes finally stopped falling. The forest was covered by a crisp, white blanket, and Scarlett the fox felt excited.

"I'll go for a walk to see how the forest looks," she said.

It was cold, and the snow came almost to the top of her legs. She loved the crunching sound it made, and the way that the whole world seemed quieter.

Soon, Scarlett spotted some birds swooping and twittering high above.

"Good evening," she called. "Isn't the snow wonderful?"

"Exciting! Exciting!" the birds chirruped. "Never seen anything like it before! Amazing! Incredible! Are you going there now?"

"Going where?" Scarlett asked. But the birds were too excited to listen. They whirled and dove and looped the loop, staying high above and far ahead.

Scarlett walked on and saw her friend Rhys the owl. He was sitting on a high tree branch, hooting to his family.

"Come on," he called. "Hurry up! I don't want to miss a moment." He looked down and spotted Scarlett.

"Hello, Scarlett. What a night! What fun!"

"Hello," Scarlett replied. "I'm going for a walk to enjoy the snow. Would you like to join me?"

Rhys jumped up and down on his branch.

"Snow?" he cried. "Never mind the snow.... There's something far more exciting to go and see!"

Suddenly, the owl's whole family started pushing out of the hole in the tree where they lived. Rhys was hidden among a flurry of soft feathers and excited hoots. Then the owls rose into the air and flew away.

"I wonder what he meant," thought
Scarlett. "Everyone is being very strange this
evening!" She started to walk faster, while overhead
more and more birds were flying in the same direction.
Then she heard voices and noticed a family of squirrels
jumping around in the snow.

"It's magical!" one of them was shouting. "Amazing!
We have to go back." Snow puffed up around the squirrels as
they leaped up and down. Scarlett ran toward them to ask
what was happening, but they bounded away, giggling and
chattering. Scarlett chased after them. She had to find out
what was making everyone so happy.

As she ran, she saw more woodland creatures fluttering and
scurrying along. Even the daytime animals were there. It was
as if everyone who lived in the forest knew what was going
on—except Scarlett.

She stopped for a moment to catch her breath.

"That's strange," she said, panting. "We're heading toward
the river, but I can't hear the water babbling and splashing
like normal."

She ran on, and when she came to the river, she understood.
It had frozen over like a skating rink! All the animals of the
forest had gathered there for a big skating party.

As the sun went down,
the animals fluffed up their fur
and feathers. They shared their food and
helped each other onto the ice. Scarlett wasn't
very good at skating at first. Her legs kept going in opposite
directions. But Rhys hovered overhead, giving her instructions,
and the other animals stayed beside her until she was spinning
and twirling across the ice.

All too soon, it was time to leave. Most of the animals had
already gone home, but Scarlett didn't want to go. She'd had
so much fun, she never wanted it to end.

"I won't forget the Big Freeze," she thought as she watched
two ducks sliding around the rink. "I hope the snow will stay
another night, so I can do it all again." (And it did.)

Oscar's Best Surprise

Oscar Bear didn't like surprises. He didn't like trying new foods in case they tasted funny. Or reading new books as he might not like the ending. Or even opening presents ... what if he didn't like the gift?

Then, one day, his mother sent him to his friend's house.

"There will be a surprise waiting when you come home," she said.

"I don't like surprises,' Oscar grumbled.

When he arrived, his friend Robyn tried to cheer Oscar up.

"There must be a surprise that you would like," she said.

She showed him a jack-in-the-box. BOING! It sprang up and made Oscar jump. Robyn laughed ... but Oscar did not.

"I don't like surprises!" he grumbled.

"Let's play a new game," Robyn said. "How about 'Please, Mr. Crocodile'?"

"I don't like new games," said Oscar. "We always play hide-and-seek."

So Oscar and Robyn played hide-and-seek. Oscar always hid in the same place, so the game was over very quickly.

When he got home, his mother waved to him from the window.

"Come in, Oscar!" she called. "The surprise is here."

So Oscar walked into the house. His mother was holding a small, soft bundle.

"Surprise, Oscar," she whispered. "You have a little brother!"

She put the warm bundle into his arms, and Oscar gazed down at the tiny baby bear. Two little eyes peeped up at him. Oscar's nose twitched, and then a big smile spread across his face. Maybe some surprises weren't so bad after all.

"You're the best baby bear in the whole world," he whispered. "I can't wait for you to meet my friend Robyn—she'll be so surprised!"

Bob Robin

Little Bob Robin,
Where do you live?
Up in yonder wood, sir,
On a hazel twig.

Can I See Another's Woe?

Can I see another's woe,
And not be in sorrow, too?
Can I see another's grief,
And not seek for kind relief?

Old Farmer Giles

Old Farmer Giles,
He went seven miles
With his faithful dog Old Rover;
And his faithful dog Old Rover,
When he came to the stiles,
Took a run, and jumped clean over.

Red Stockings

Red stockings, blue stockings,
Shoes tied up with silver;
A red rosette upon my breast
And a gold ring on my finger.

The Dove Says

The dove says, "Coo, coo! What shall I do?
I can scarce maintain two."
"Pooh, pooh," says the wren, "I have ten,
And keep them all like gentlemen.
Curr dhoo, curr dhoo! Love me and I'll love you!"

Fidget

As little Jenny Wren
Was sitting by the shed,
She waggled with her tail,
She nodded with her head;
She waggled with her tail,
She nodded with her head;
As Little Jenny Wren
Was sitting by the shed.

The Moonlight Tooth Fairy

Twinkle was a tooth fairy. Every night, she flew from house to house collecting the teeth that children had left under their pillows.

Each time she took a tooth, she slipped a shiny coin in its place.

Twinkle loved to make people happy, but she often felt lonely.

"I wish I had a friend," she thought.

One night, Twinkle visited Lisa's house. As she flew through the open window she felt somebody watching her. A fairy face stared at her in the moonlight. And another. There were fairy pictures and toys everywhere!

Twinkle was so surprised, she dropped the coin. The noise woke Lisa.

Lisa gasped when she spotted Twinkle.

Twinkle started to cry. "You've seen me! I've broken the most important fairy rule!"

"Don't cry!" said Lisa, gazing at Twinkle in amazement. "I won't tell anyone, I promise."

"And I've lost your coin!" sobbed Twinkle.

Lisa had an idea. "Instead of giving me a coin, could you grant me a fairy wish?" she asked.

"What would you wish for?" said Twinkle, drying her tears.

"I wish to be a fairy just like you!"

Twinkle waved magic into the room. Suddenly, Lisa felt herself shrinking.

"I'm growing wings!" she cried with joy. "Will you teach me how to fly?"

"It's easy!" said Twinkle. "Hold my hand…."

Twinkle led Lisa out into the moonlit garden. They flew between the trees and skimmed a starry pond.

"I love being a fairy!" cried Lisa.

"It's much more fun with two," laughed Twinkle happily. At last she had a real friend of her own.

Soon it was time for Lisa to go back to being a little girl. "Thank you for making my wish come true," she said to Twinkle.

"You've made my wish come true, too!" replied Twinkle.

Twinkle promised to come back soon.

As she flew away, she whispered, "Sweet dreams, my fairy friend!"

Here We Go Round the Mulberry Bush

Here we go round the mulberry bush,
The mulberry bush, the mulberry bush,
Here we go round the mulberry bush,
On a cold and frosty morning.

This is the way we wash our hands,
Wash our hands, wash our hands,
This is the way we wash our hands,
On a cold and frosty morning.

This is the way we wash our clothes,
Wash our clothes, wash our clothes,
This is the way we wash our clothes,
On a cold and frosty morning.

Here we go round the mulberry bush,
The mulberry bush, the mulberry bush,
Here we go round the mulberry bush,
On a cold and frosty morning.

Where Are You Going to,
My Pretty Maid?

Where are you going to, my pretty maid?
Where are you going to, my pretty maid?
    I'm going a-milking, sir, she said,
      Sir, she said, sir, she said,
    I'm going a-milking, sir, she said.

May I go with you, my pretty maid?
May I go with you, my pretty maid?
    You're kindly welcome, sir, she said,
      Sir, she said, sir, she said,
    You're kindly welcome, sir, she said.

What is your fortune, my pretty maid?
What is your fortune, my pretty maid?
    My face is my fortune, sir, she said,
      Sir, she said, sir, she said,
    My face is my fortune, sir, she said.

Then I can't marry you, my pretty maid,
Then I can't marry you, my pretty maid,
    Nobody asked you, sir, she said,
      Sir, she said, sir, she said,
    Nobody asked you, sir, she said.

I'm a Big Sister!

Ellie was Mommy's and Daddy's little girl. But one day, Mommy went into hospital ... and when she came back, she had a new baby with her.

"Now you're a big sister!" Mommy told Ellie.

Everyone made a big fuss of the new baby.

"Baby's so little!" Auntie Molly said. "Isn't it lovely to be a big sister?"

"Yes," said Ellie. But she wasn't so sure. Sometimes she wished she could be little again, like Baby.

When Baby's diaper needed changing, Ellie asked Mommy, "Did I wear a diaper too?"

Mommy smiled. "Yes, you did, Ellie. But now you're too grown-up for diapers. Big sisters wear underpants. Yours have flowers on them."

"And I can put them on myself," said Ellie.

"That's right," said Mommy. "But Baby still needs lots of help, not like you!"

"Can I help change Baby's diaper?" Ellie asked.

"Of course," said Mommy. "Thank you. Baby's very lucky to have a big sister who helps!"

But Ellie still thought it might be fun to be as little as Baby.

The next day, when Daddy got the baby's bottle ready, Ellie asked, "Did I have my dinner in a bottle too?"

Daddy smiled. "Yes, Ellie," he said. "But now you're too grown-up for a bottle. Big sisters eat sandwiches and drink milk from a cup."

"And I can eat sandwiches and drink milk all by myself!" said Ellie. "I don't need anyone to help me."

"Of course you can," said Daddy. "That's what big sisters do. But Baby still needs lots of help."

"Can I help feed the baby?" Ellie asked Daddy.

"I think Baby would like that very much," said Daddy. "Baby's so lucky to have such a helpful big sister!"

That night, Ellie watched Mommy put Baby to sleep.

"Did I sleep in a crib like Baby's?" she asked.

"Yes, Ellie, you did. But now you're too grown-up for a crib," said Mommy. "Big sisters sleep in big, cozy beds, just like yours."

Ellie looked at her bed. With its pretty quilt and a huge pile of cuddly toys, it really did look cozy.

"There are no animals in Baby's crib," Ellie said. "Let's give Baby my yellow bunny, just for now."

"That's very kind of you, Ellie," said Mommy. "Baby is lucky to have a big sister who shares!"

The next day, Ellie and Mommy went out to the park. Baby came too, in a stroller.

"Did I ride in a stroller like Baby?" Ellie asked.

"Yes, you did," replied Mommy. "But you're a big sister now. Big sisters can walk, and run and jump. Baby can't do any of those things yet. Baby's lucky to have a strong big sister like you!"

At the park, Ellie saw the ice-cream truck.

"Will you buy an ice cream for Baby?" she asked Mommy.

"No, Ellie," said Mommy. "Baby's too little for ice cream.
But her big sister isn't! What flavor would you like?"

"Chocolate!" said Ellie. "Thank you!"

Ellie looked at Baby, and Baby smiled at her.

Ellie smiled too.

"I'm glad we have a baby," she told Mommy. "I get to help,
and share and push the stroller, and I get to have ice cream
too! Being a big sister is the best!"

The Dame of Dundee

There was an old woman,
Who lived in Dundee,
And in her back garden
There was a plum tree;
The plums they grew rotten
Before they grew ripe,
And she sold them
Three farthings a pint.

Tinker, Tailor

Tinker, tailor,
Soldier, sailor!

Mrs. Mason's Basin

Mrs. Mason bought a basin.
Mrs. Tyson said, "What a nice one!"
"What did it cost?" asked Mrs. Frost,
"Half a crown," said Mrs. Brown,
"Did it indeed?" said Mrs. Reed,
"It did for certain," said Mrs. Burton.
Then Mrs. Nix, up to her tricks,
Threw the basin on the bricks.

The Merchants of London

Hey diddle dinkety, poppety pet,
The merchants of London they wear scarlet;
Silk in the collar and gold in the hem,
So merrily march the merchant men.

My Maid Mary

My maid Mary,
She tends the dairy,
While I go a-hoeing and mowing each morn;
Merrily runs the reel,
And the little spinning wheel,
While I am singing and mowing my corn.

Grandma's Glasses

These are Grandma's glasses,
This is Grandma's hat;
Grandma claps her hands like this,
And rests them in her lap.

These are Grandpa's glasses,
This is Grandpa's hat;
Grandpa folds his arms like this,
And has a little nap.

Rebecca Rabbit's Birthday Wish

Rebecca Rabbit had just one wish for her birthday. She didn't want presents or even a party.

"Please, please, please," she whispered, "let me have the biggest carrot cake in the world!" But Rebecca was so busy wishing for the cake that she forgot to tell her friends that *this* was what she really wanted.

On the day of Rebecca's birthday, her friends surprised her with a big party. There were piles of presents and sparkling party hats. But she couldn't see a single cake. Rebecca couldn't help feeling a tiny bit disappointed. She didn't see her friends smiling and winking at each other.

First, Rosie Rabbit held out a very large box. When Rebecca opened it, she found a big cake inside. It was lovely, but it had only one layer.

"Thank you," said Rebecca with a smile.

It wasn't the enormous cake she had dreamed about, but it looked delicious. She knew that Rosie must have worked really hard to bake it.

Then Rex Rabbit held out his present. Rebecca opened it and found another cake, a little smaller than the first.

"I can put it on top of the other cake," she said, starting to feel really excited. Her birthday cake would have two tiers!

One by one, she opened her presents, and each one was a new cake. Hopping with excitement, Rebecca placed them one on top of the other, until the cake was towering above her.

"It really is the biggest carrot cake in the world!" she whispered.

Then, when her friends sang "Happy Birthday," Rebecca climbed to the top of the cake and blew out her candles. But she didn't make a wish.

"I already have everything I want ..." she said happily, "an enormous cake and the greatest friends in the world! Thank you, everyone."

Bird Bear

Isla was a little bear cub. She lived in the woods with her mommy and daddy, and her big sister. One day, she was playing with her sister when she saw some blue tits swooping out of their nest, high up in a tree. Isla stared at the birds as they glided and fluttered and flew. Then she gave a deep, long sigh.

"I want to fly like that," she said.

"Bears can't fly," said her sister.

"Then I don't want to be a bear anymore," Isla said. "I want to be a blue tit and fly through the sky, and live in a nest in a tree."

Isla's sister just shook her head. She knew that bears couldn't turn into birds. But Isla couldn't stop thinking about it. She climbed up the tree and watched the birds all afternoon. Her sister got fed up and wandered off, but Isla didn't care.

"Birds have wings," she said to herself. "If I make myself some wings, maybe I'll be able to fly too."

She pulled two leafy branches off the tree and climbed down. Holding one in each hand, Isla started to run, flapping the branches up and down as fast as she could. But she didn't raise a single toe off the ground. Feeling gloomy, she walked back toward home, trailing the branches behind her.

On the way, Isla spotted a finch pecking the ground. As she watched, the finch pulled a worm out of the ground and swallowed it whole. Then it flew away.

"Hmm," said Isla. "Perhaps I need to learn to be a bird in other ways before I can fly."

She dropped the branches and knelt down on the ground. After a long wait, she saw a worm poking through the soil. With a single gulp, she swallowed it down. It tasted horrible!

"Yuck!" she growled. "Yuck! Yuck! Yuck! Why do birds eat worms? Someone should tell them about honey!"

Just then, a blackbird nearby started to sing.

"That's it!" Isla exclaimed. "I will learn to sing as sweetly as a bird!"

She opened her mouth as wide as it would go, and began to sing in her highest voice.

"ARRRGHHH! EEEEEE! OOOOOOH!" All the animals nearby dove for cover. The birds shot up out of the trees in fright. A rabbit poked her head out of a hole in the ground and glared at Isla.

"Stop making that awful noise!" she snapped. "My babies are asleep!"

"I'm sorry," said Isla. "I was trying to sing like a bird."

"Well, it didn't work," said the rabbit in a cross voice. "If I were you, I'd stop trying to be something you're not."

Suddenly, Isla felt very tired. She was about to sit down when she saw her mommy gathering honeycombs for supper. She clambered onto mommy's back and held on tight.

"What a tired bear," said her mommy. "Have you had a busy day?"

"Very busy," said Isla, yawning. "Mommy, why can't I be a bird and fly around?"

"Because you're a bear cub, and that's what you do best," said her mommy. "Now, shall I carry you home and tell you all about the trees we're going to climb tomorrow? I know where to find all the biggest honeycombs."

Isla nodded and snuggled into her mommy's cozy fur.

Night started to fall, and the moon came out. Isla yawned again. She still thought that being able to fly like a bird would be wonderful. But being able to climb trees and eat honeycombs with her mommy was even better!

I Want to Be TALL!

Delilah was a little dinosaur. She lived in a cozy cave with her mom and dad and had a happy life. But there was one thing Delilah wished for more than anything else....

She wanted to be TALL!

"It's not fair!" cried Delilah, stamping her little feet. "I can't reach the juicy fruits and leaves at the tops of the trees."

"You will be able to one day, Delilah," soothed Mommy. "You just have to wait to grow up."

"But I want to be tall NOW!" roared Delilah crossly. "I want to be taller than the trees."

"You might bump your head on the ceiling if you get that tall!" laughed Daddy.

"Better than being this small," Delilah thought grumpily to herself. Surely there must be a way of getting taller quicker.

Delilah tried jumping high into the sky.

She tried stretching her arms up.

She even ate all her vegetables, because Mommy said they would make her grow big and strong.

But nothing seemed to work.

One evening, Delilah went for a walk with Daddy.

"I wish I was tall enough to reach the stars!" sighed Delilah. "If only I was taller than …"

RRRRRROAR!

"What's that?" screamed Delilah, as a giant creature came rushing out of the trees.

"Run, Delilah!" shouted Daddy. "It's a Tyrannosaurus Rex!"

As Delilah dashed after Daddy, she spied a small opening in the rocky cliff up ahead.

"Daddy, quick! Let's hide in here," cried Delilah.

Delilah and Daddy squeezed into the small dark cave. Outside, the huge T-Rex roared in frustration. He was too tall to fit through the gap in the rocks.

Daddy hugged Delilah close. "Well done, Delilah—you saved us!"

Delilah grinned up at Daddy.

"Perhaps being small isn't so bad after all," she laughed.

Arabella Miller

Little Arabella Miller found a hairy caterpillar.
First it crawled upon her mother,
Then upon her baby brother.
All said, "Arabella Miller, take away that caterpillar!"

Oats and Beans and Barley Grow

Oats and beans and barley grow,
Oats and beans and barley grow.
Do you or I or anyone know
How oats and beans and barley grow?

First the farmer sows his seed,
Then he stands and takes his ease.
He stamps his feet and claps his hands
And turns around to view the lands.

Each Peach, Pear, Plum

Each peach, pear, plum, out goes Tom Thumb;
Tom Thumb won't do, out goes Betty Blue;
Betty Blue won't go, so out goes you.

Peter, Peter

Peter, Peter, pumpkin eater,
Had a wife and couldn't keep her.
He put her in a pumpkin shell
And there he kept her very well.

Monday's Child

Monday's child is fair of face,
Tuesday's child is full of grace,
Wednesday's child is full of woe,
Thursday's child has far to go,
Friday's child is loving and giving,
Saturday's child works hard for his living,
And the child that is born on the Sabbath day
Is bonny and blithe and good and gay.

Lavender's Blue

Lavender's blue, dilly, dilly,
Lavender's green;
When I am king, dilly, dilly,
You shall be queen.

The Fox and the Crow

One day, a crow was flying past an open window when she spotted a tasty piece of cheese on the table. There was no one in the room, so she fluttered in and stole it! Then she flew up into the branches of a nearby tree, and was just about to eat the cheese when a fox appeared.

The fox was also particularly fond of cheese, and he was determined to steal the crow's prize.

"Good morning, Mistress Crow," he greeted her. "May I say that you are looking especially beautiful today? Your feathers are so glossy, and your eyes are as bright as sparkling jewels!"

The fox hoped that the crow would reply and drop the cheese, but she didn't even thank him for his compliments. So he tried again: "You have such a graceful neck, and your claws are really magnificent. They look like the claws of an eagle."

Still the crow ignored him.

The fox could smell the delicious cheese, and it was making his mouth water. He had to find a way to make the crow drop it.

At last he came up with a plan.

"All in all, you are a most beautiful bird," he said. "In fact, if your voice matched your beauty, I would call you the Queen of Birds. Why don't you sing a song for me?"

Now, the crow liked the idea of being addressed as the Queen of Birds by all the other creatures in the woods. She thought that the fox would be very impressed by her loud voice, so she lifted her head and started to caw.

Of course, as soon as she opened her beak, the piece of cheese fell down, down, down to the ground. The fox grabbed it in a flash and gobbled it up.

"Thank you," he said. "That was all I wanted. I have to say that you may have a loud voice, but you don't have a very good brain!"

And the moral of the story is: Be wary of a flatterer.

The Swing

How do you like to go up in a swing,
Up in the air so blue?
Oh, I do think it the pleasantest thing
Ever a child can do!

Up in the air and over the wall,
Till I can see so wide,
River and trees and cattle and all
Over the countryside—

Till I look down on the garden green,
Down on the roof so brown—
Up in the air I go flying again,
Up in the air and down!

City Child

Dainty little maiden, whither would you wander?
Whither from this pretty home, the home where mother dwells?
"Far and far away," said the dainty little maiden,
"All among the gardens, auriculas, anemones,
Roses and lilies and Canterbury bells."

Dainty little maiden, whither would you wander?
Whither from this pretty house, this city house of ours?
"Far and far away," said the dainty little maiden,
"All among the meadows, the clover and the clematis,
Daisies and kingcups and honeysuckle flowers."

The Fisherman and His Wife

One day, when the sea was blue and calm, a poor fisherman set off to work. At first, he caught nothing. Then, when the fisherman was about to call it a day, he felt a tug on his line. The fisherman struggled to reel it in.

"This must be a big fish," he thought.

The fish was enormous, and the fisherman was very pleased. But his pleasure turned to surprise when the fish spoke to him.

"Please throw me back," pleaded the fish. "I am not really a fish at all, but an enchanted prince."

The stunned fisherman gently let the fish back into the water and set off for home.

The fisherman and his wife were so poor that they lived in a wooden shed. When he told his wife about the talking fish, she was angry with him.

"You fool!" she cried. "No wonder we're so poor, if you can't see a good thing when it's biting you on the nose!"

The fisherman's wife told him that if the fish was an enchanted prince, he should have asked for something in return for setting him free.

"Go back to the same spot tomorrow and catch that fish again, and this time ask him for a little cottage so we can live a better life," said the fisherman's wife.

The next morning, when the sea was green and choppy, the fisherman set off again. He rowed out to the same spot as the day before, hoping to see the magical fish.

"Enchanted prince, please hear my plea, jump out from the water and talk to me," called the fisherman.

The fish appeared and asked the fisherman why he had called him. The fisherman explained that he was a very poor man and would like to live in a little cottage instead of a wooden shed.

"Go home," said the fish. "Your wish is granted." And he left with a SPLISH!

So the fisherman returned to his wife, who waved to him from the window of their lovely new cottage.

The fisherman's wife was pleased for a little while, but soon became unhappy again.

"We could have asked for more from that magic fish," she told her husband one evening. "This is only a small cottage; a castle would be much better." And she begged her husband to go and find the magical fish, and ask him to grant her wish.

The next morning, when the sea was purple and rough, the fisherman set off again and rowed out to the same spot as before.

"Enchanted prince, please hear my plea, jump out from the water and talk to me," called the fisherman.

The fish appeared, although he didn't seem very happy about being called again. The fisherman explained that his wife found the cottage rather small, and would prefer to live in a castle.

"Go home," said the fish. "Your wish is granted." And he left with a SPLASH!

So the fisherman returned to his wife, who waved to him from the window of a grand castle.

But the fisherman's wife wanted even more. "If that fish can give us a grand castle, he can make me a queen," she said.

The next morning, when the sea was gray and murky, the fisherman set off again and rowed out to the same spot as before.

"Enchanted prince, please hear my plea, jump out from the water and talk to me," called the fisherman.

The fish appeared, not at all pleased to be called again. The fisherman explained that his wife now wanted to be a queen.

"Go home," said the fish. "Your wish is granted." And he left with a SPLOSH!

So the fisherman returned to his wife, now a queen.

"If that fish can make me a queen, then he can make me the ruler of the whole world!" said the fisherman's wife.

The next morning, when the sea was black and stormy, the fisherman rowed out to the same spot as before.

"Enchanted prince, please hear my plea, jump out from the water and talk to me," called the fisherman.

The fish appeared. He was furious. The fisherman explained that his wife now wanted to be the ruler of the world.

"Go home," said the fish. "Your wife has what she deserves." And he left with a SPLISH, SPLASH, SPLOSH!

The fisherman returned to his wife ... who was living in the wooden shed again.

Her greed had indeed been rewarded!

Old King Cole

Old King Cole was a merry old soul,
And a merry old soul was he.
He called for his pipe in the middle of the night,
And he called for his fiddlers three.
Every fiddler had a very fine fiddle,
And a very fine fiddle had he.
Oh, there's none so rare as can compare,
With King Cole and his fiddlers three.

Hector Protector

Hector Protector was dressed all in green;
Hector Protector was sent to the Queen.
The Queen did not like him,
No more did the King;
So Hector Protector was sent back again.

There Was an Old Man from Peru

There was an old man from Peru
Who dreamed he was eating his shoe.
He woke in a fright
In the middle of the night
And found it was perfectly true.

How Many Miles to Babylon?

How many miles to Babylon?
Three score miles and ten.
Can I get there by candlelight?
Yes, and back again.
If your heels are nimble and light,
You may get there by candlelight.

BABYLON

Cinderella

Once upon a time, there was a young girl who lived with her father, stepmother and two stepsisters. The stepmother was unkind, and the stepsisters were mean. They made the girl do all the housework, eat scraps, and sleep by the fireplace among the cinders and ashes. Because she was always covered with cinders, they called her "Cinderella".

One morning, a special invitation arrived. All the young women in the kingdom were invited to a royal ball—a ball for the prince to choose a bride!

Cinderella longed to go, but her stepsisters just laughed.

"You? Go to a ball? In those rags? How ridiculous!" they cackled.

Instead, Cinderella had to rush around helping her stepsisters get ready for the ball.

As they left for the palace, Cinderella sat beside the fireplace and wept.

"I wish I could go to the ball," she cried.

Suddenly, a sparkle of light filled the dull kitchen, and a fairy appeared!

"Don't be afraid, my dear," she said. "I am your fairy godmother, and you SHALL go to the ball!"

"But how?" said Cinderella.

"Find me a big pumpkin, four white mice, and a rat," replied the fairy godmother.

Cinderella found everything as quickly as she could. The fairy godmother waved her wand, and the pumpkin changed into a magnificent golden coach, the white mice became white horses, and the rat became a coachman.

With one last gentle tap of her wand, the fairy godmother changed Cinderella's dusty dress into a shimmering ball gown. On her feet were two sparkling glass slippers.

"Now, off you go," said the fairy godmother, "but remember, all this will vanish at midnight, so make sure you are home by then."

Cinderella climbed into the coach, and it whisked her away to the palace.

Everyone was enchanted by the lovely stranger, especially the prince, who danced with her all evening. As Cinderella whirled around the room in his arms, she felt so happy that she completely forgot her fairy godmother's warning.

Suddenly, she heard the clock strike midnight....

BONG ... BONG ... BONG....

Cinderella picked up her
skirt and fled from the ballroom.
The worried prince ran after her.

BONG ... BONG ... BONG....
She ran down the palace steps, losing
a glass slipper on the way, but she didn't
dare stop.

BONG ... BONG ... BONG....
Cinderella jumped into the
coach, and it drove off
before he could stop her.

BONG ... BONG ... BONG!
On the final stroke of midnight,
Cinderella found herself sitting on the road beside a pumpkin,
four white mice, and a black rat. She was dressed in rags and
had only a single glass slipper left from her magical evening.

At the palace, the prince saw something twinkling on the
steps—a single glass slipper!

"I will marry the woman whose foot fits this glass slipper,"
he declared.

The next day, the prince took the glass slipper and visited
every house in the kingdom.

At last, the prince came to Cinderella's house. Her stepsisters tried and tried to squeeze their huge feet into the delicate slipper, but no matter what they did, they could not get the slipper to fit. Cinderella watched as she scrubbed the floor.

"May I try, please?" she asked.

"You didn't even go to the ball!" laughed the elder stepsister.

"Everyone may try," said the prince, as he held out the sparkling slipper. And suddenly ...

"Oh!" gasped the stepsisters, as Cinderella's dainty foot slipped easily into it.

The prince joyfully took Cinderella in his arms.

"Will you marry me?" he asked.

"I will!" Cinderella said.

Much to the disgust of her stepmother and stepsisters, soon Cinderella and the prince were married.

They lived long, happy lives together, and Cinderella's stepmother and stepsisters had to do their own cleaning and never went to a royal ball again.

Ariel's Song

Full fathom five thy father lies;
Of his bones are coral made;
Those are pearls that were his eyes:
Nothing of him that doth fade,
But doth suffer a sea-change
Into something rich and strange.
Sea nymphs hourly ring his knell:
Ding-dong!
Hark! Now I hear them,
Ding-dong, bell!

Ickle Ockle

Ickle ockle, blue bockle,
Fishes in the sea,
If you want a pretty maid,
Please choose me.

Little Fishes

Little fishes in a brook,
Father caught them on a hook,
Mother fried them in a pan,
Johnnie eats them like a man.

Maddie's Mistake

It was Maddie the Mermaid's birthday, and she was having a party. She had made jellyfish jelly, octopus ink drink, and seaweed cake. And, like all mermaids, she would get a magical birthday wish.

"The cake looks delicious," said Maddie. "But I'd better check." She had a little nibble. Then another ... and another.

"I'll just make sure it tastes the same all over," she said.

Before she knew it, all the cake had gone. What a disaster! The guests would arrive soon. Then Maddie remembered her wish.

"I don't need a present," she whispered. "My magical birthday wish is a big, beautiful cake."

A huge seaweed cake with blue frosting appeared. When the guests arrived, Maddie cut it up and handed a slice to each guest. But she didn't have a single piece. She'd had quite enough cake for one day!

Alice and the White Rabbit

One day, Alice was sitting beside a river with her sister when something curious happened—a white rabbit with pink eyes ran past.

"Oh dear! Oh dear! I shall be too late!" he said. Then he took a watch out of his vest pocket and hurried on.

Alice followed the rabbit down a large rabbit hole. It went straight on like a tunnel for some way and then dipped so suddenly that she found herself falling down....

"I must be getting near the center of the Earth," Alice thought to herself. Down, down, down Alice kept falling.

Suddenly, she landed in a heap at the bottom. When she got up, she found herself in a long hall, lined with doors. At the end was a little three-legged glass table. There was nothing on it but a tiny golden key. Alice tried the key in all the doors, but it wouldn't open any of them.

Then she noticed a low curtain she had not seen before. Behind it was a tiny door.

She turned the key in the lock, and it opened. The door led into a beautiful garden, but Alice could not even get her head through the doorway.

She went back to the table and saw a little bottle labeled "DRINK ME!"

Alice drank it and shrank. But she remembered that she had left the key on the table. Alice didn't know what to do. Then, she saw a cake marked "EAT ME!"

Alice ate it and began to grow. Soon, she was so large that her head touched the ceiling!

Alice began to cry. She was wondering what to do, when who should come along but the white rabbit? He was carrying a pair of white gloves and a large fan.

"If you please, sir …" began Alice.

The rabbit dropped the gloves and fan, and scurried away.

"How strange everything is today," said Alice, picking up the gloves and the fan. "I'm not myself at all." Then she began fanning herself as she wondered who she might be instead.

After a while, Alice looked down at her hands. She was surprised to see that she had put on one of the rabbit's little white gloves.

"I must be growing smaller again," she thought.

Alice realized that it was the fan that was making her shrink, so she dropped it quickly and ran to the door. Suddenly, she remembered that the key was still on the table.

"Drat," she said. "Things can't possibly get any worse." But she was wrong. SPLASH! She fell into a sea of her tears.

"I wish I hadn't cried so much!" wailed Alice.

Just then, she heard something splashing. It was a mouse.

"Do you know the way out of this pool?" asked Alice.

The mouse didn't reply.

"Perhaps he speaks French," thought Alice. So she began again. "Où est mon chat?" which was the first sentence in her French book and meant "Where is my cat?"

The mouse leaped out of the water in fright.

"I'm sorry!" cried Alice. "I didn't mean to scare you."

"Come ashore," said the mouse. "I'll tell you why cats frighten me."

By this time, the pool was crowded with birds and animals. There was a duck, a dodo, a parrot, an eaglet, and other curious creatures too. Together, they all swam to the shore.

The birds and animals were dripping wet.

"Let's have a race," said the dodo. "It will help us dry off." And he began to mark out a course.

Then everyone began, starting and stopping whenever they felt like it. It was impossible to tell when the race was over, but after half an hour they were all very dry.

"But who won the race?" asked the mouse.

"Everyone," said the dodo. "Alice will give out prizes." So Alice handed around some candies she had in her pocket.

"But she must have a prize, too," said the mouse.

"What else do you have in your pocket?" asked the dodo.

Alice handed over a thimble and he gave it back to her, saying, "I beg you to accept this thimble."

Alice accepted as solemnly as she could, and then they all sat down to hear the mouse's tale. But Alice was so tired, she just couldn't concentrate, and she drifted off to sleep.

The next moment, she woke to the sound of her sister's voice. "Wake up, Alice!" said her sister. "What a long sleep you've had!"

"I've had such a curious dream!" said Alice, who told her sister all about it. And what a wonderful dream it had been!

The Loudest ROAR!

Leo the little lion cub wanted to be just like Daddy when he grew up.

"I'm going to have the loudest ROAR ever!" he said.

Daddy Lion grinned and patted Leo gently on the head with his large paw.

"Yes, one day you will," he said. "But while you are still little, why don't we go and play?"

"Teach me to roar like you first, Daddy, please!" pleaded Leo. He opened his little mouth but ...

"GRRRRR!"

Leo could only make a tiny growling sound. The little lion cub stomped his paws on the ground in frustration.

"It needs to be louder, Daddy!" he cried.

Daddy lion smiled. "Don't worry, Leo, it will get louder with practice." Then he opened his mouth wide....

"RRRRRRROAR!"

The roar was so loud that the ground trembled under Leo's paws!

"GRRRRR!" Leo tried again.

"Sit up straight and tip your head back," advised Daddy. "And then open your mouth as wide as it will go...."

Leo watched Daddy lion closely. He sat up straight, tipped his head back and opened his mouth as wide as it would go....

"RRRRRROAR!"

Leo could feel the ground trembling under his paws.

"That's my boy!" laughed Daddy. "You've got it!"

Leo was so happy with his new roar that he practiced it all afternoon. Soon he was exhausted.

"That's enough for today," said Daddy as he settled Leo down for bed. "You don't want to lose your voice."

But Leo didn't hear him. He was already fast asleep, dreaming about his wonderful new loud roar!

Bread and Milk for Breakfast

Bread and milk for breakfast,
And woollen frocks to wear,
And a crumb for robin redbreast
On the cold days of the year.

Spin, Dame

Spin, Dame, spin,
Your bread you must win;
Twist the thread and break it not,
Spin, Dame, spin.

Little Tommy Tucker

Little Tommy Tucker
Sings for his supper:
What shall we give him?
Brown bread and butter.
How shall he cut it
Without a knife?
How can he marry
Without a wife?

One Misty, Moisty Morning

One misty, moisty morning,
When cloudy was the weather;
There I met an old man
All clothed in leather.
He began to compliment
And I began to grin;
How do you do?
And how do you do?
And how do you do again?

A-tisket, A-tasket

A-tisket, a-tasket,
A green and yellow basket.
I wrote a letter to my love,
And on the way I dropped it.
I dropped it, I dropped it,
And on the way I dropped it.
A little boy picked it up,
And put it in his pocket.

Cobbler, Cobbler

Cobbler, cobbler, mend my shoe,
Get it done by half past two.
Half past two is much too late!
Get it done by half past eight.

Home Hunt

Florence and Noah were space adventurers. They zoomed around the galaxy in their rocket, searching for the perfect place to call home.

"Let's visit that one!" said Florence, pointing at a red planet. "Engage landing rockets!"

They landed the rocket and stepped out onto the planet. It was very dusty, and there was a big sign saying "Welcome to Mars." The sign needed a good polishing.

"I wonder who lives here," said Noah.

Just then, a small, green alien with five arms, six legs, and no eyebrows came hurrying up to them.

"Greetings, and welcome to Mars," said the alien. "We hope you enjoy your visit. Please have a welcome snack."

He handed them each a green blob with pink spots on it. The children wanted to be polite, so they ate the blobs, which tasted a lot like boiled grass.

"Would you like to come and play?" asked the alien. "We're in the middle of our favorite game. It's called Shiver My Collywobbles."

"How do you play?" asked Noah.

"Everyone has to stand on the spot and shake," the alien explained. "Whoever can shake the longest is the winner. We're on day seven, and no one's given up yet. It really is very exciting!"

Florence and Noah looked at each other. Neither of them liked the sound of that.

"We have to go now," said Florence. "But thank you for asking us."

They blasted off from Mars and flew on until they saw a beautiful shining moon.

"Time for a moon landing!" said Noah. Their rocket bumped down into a crater, and they climbed out. A small pink alien was waiting for them. She had one eye and a very friendly smile.

"Welcome to the Moon," she said. "Unlike other moons, we welcome visitors and have lots of things to do. Please feel free to add your flag to our collection."

"We don't have a flag," said Florence. "But we'd love to look around."

Welcome to Mars

The alien was proud of her home and showed them everything. They rowed a boat across Lunar Lake. They bounced on crater trampolines. They played catch with the pink aliens (but it wasn't much fun because the pink aliens didn't have arms).

Then Florence looked up and saw a green-and-blue planet shining out in space.

"Wow!" she said. "What a beautiful planet! I wonder what sort of aliens live there."

She and Noah said goodbye to the moon aliens and jumped into their rocket.

Three . . . two . . . one . . . BLAST OFF!

Florence and Noah landed on Earth in the middle of a playground. When they peeped out of their rocket, several children were peering back at them.

"They look just like us," said Florence.

Noah waved, and the children smiled and waved back.

"Come and play!" they called. At first, Florence and Noah were worried about the strange games they might play. But when they joined in, they realized that the games were fun!

They flew kites and rode bikes. They tried the swings and played ball. But best of all, they made lots of new friends.

When the children were called in for lunch, Florence and Noah looked at each other.

"I love it here," Florence whispered.

"Let's stay," said Noah.

Their new friends cheered and clapped.

"Welcome to Earth," they shouted. "There's no place like it!"

Bye Baby Bunting

Bye baby bunting,
Daddy's gone a-hunting,
To get a little rabbit skin
To wrap his baby bunting in.

Hush-a-bye, Baby

Hush-a-bye, baby, on the treetop,
When the wind blows the cradle will rock;
When the bough breaks the cradle will fall,
And down will come baby, cradle and all.

A Star

I have a little sister, they call her Peep, Peep;
She wades the waters deep, deep, deep;
She climbs the mountains high, high, high;
Poor little creature, she has but one eye.

Nothing-at-all

There was an old woman called Nothing-at-all,
Who rejoiced in a dwelling exceedingly small;
A man stretched his mouth to its utmost extent,
And down at one gulp house and old woman went.

There Was an Old Woman Had Three Sons

There was an old woman had three sons,
Jerry and James and John:
Jerry was hung, James was drowned,
John was lost and never was found,
And there was an end of the three sons,
Jerry and James and John!

Old Mother Goose

Old Mother Goose,
When she wanted to wander,
Would ride through the air
On a very fine gander.

The Fox and the Stork

Once upon a time, a fox decided to play a trick on his neighbor, the stork.

"Would you like to come and have supper with me?" he asked her one morning.

The stork was surprised by the invitation, because the fox had never been friendly to her before, but she happily accepted. He looked like a well-fed beast, and she was sure he would provide her with a good meal.

Every now and then, through the day, the stork caught the mouth-watering smell of the soup that the fox was preparing. By the time she arrived at his home, she was feeling very hungry—which was exactly what the fox wanted.

"Enjoy your meal," said the crafty fox, ladling the soup into a shallow bowl.

Of course, the fox was able to lap his up easily, but the stork could only dip the tip of her bill into the soup. She wasn't able to drink a single drop!

"Mmm, that was delicious," said the fox when he had slurped up the soup. "I see you don't have much of an appetite, so I will have yours, too."

The poor stork went home feeling hungrier than ever and was determined to take her revenge on the sly fox for playing such a mean trick. So, the following week, she went to see him.

"Thank you for inviting me to supper last week," she said. "Now I would like to return the favor. Please come and dine with me this evening."

The fox was a little suspicious that the stork might want to get back at him, but he didn't see how she could possibly play a trick on him. After all, he was known for his cunning, and very few creatures had ever managed to outwit him.

All day long the fox looked forward to his supper, and by the evening he was very hungry. As he approached the stork's home he caught the appetizing aroma of a fish stew and started to lick his lips.

But when the stork served the stew it was in a tall pot with a very narrow neck. The stork could reach the food easily with her long bill, but the fox could only lick the rim of the pot and sniff the tempting smell. As much as he didn't want to, the fox had to admit he had been outsmarted— and he went home with an empty stomach!

Engine, Engine

Engine, engine, number nine,
Running on the Chicago line;
When she's polished she will shine,
Engine, engine, number nine.

Puss at the Door

Who's that ringing at my doorbell?
A little pussycat that isn't very well.
Rub its little nose with a little mutton fat,
That's the best cure for a little pussycat.

Buff

I had a dog
Whose name was Buff,
I sent him for
A bag of snuff;
He broke the bag
And spilled the stuff,
And that was all
My penny's-worth.

The Gossips

Miss One, Two and Three
Could never agree,
While they gossiped around
A tea-caddy.

Three Ghostesses

Three little ghostesses,
Sitting on postesses,
Eating buttered toastesses,
Greasing their fistesses,
Up to their wristesses.
Oh what beastesses
To make such feastesses!

Washing Day

The old woman must stand
At the tub, tub, tub,
The dirty clothes to rub, rub, rub;
But when they are clean,
And fit to be seen,
She'll dress like a lady
And dance on the green.

Ella's Year

Ella's daddy always moaned about the weather.

"It's too windy," he grumbled in spring. Ella laughed.

"Wind is fun," she said, helping him fly a kite high in the air.

In summer, Daddy didn't want to play outside.

"It's too hot," he said. "I need to cool down."

"Sunny days are fun," said Ella. She held Daddy's hand and they ran to the cool, blue sea for a splash and a paddle.

When fall came, Daddy frowned.

"The fallen leaves are too messy," he complained.

"They're beautiful," said Ella. She showed him how to rustle and crunch through the leaves on the walk to school.

Soon, winter arrived.

"It's too cold," said Daddy. "There's nothing good about winter."

"Winter is the best season of all," said Ella, and she pulled him outside to build a snowman.

Daddy laughed. "I may not always like the weather," he said, "but I love playing with you, Ella!"

378

Rosie's Surprise

Rosie longed to ride a horse at the stables, just like her brother, Ben. But Ben only let his sister clean out the stalls.

"You don't know anything about horses," he told her. "You can watch me ride while you clean."

Then, one morning, when Ben was trying to ride his newest horse, it refused to budge or do anything it was told.

"I bet I can help," thought Rosie.

So the next day, she got up early and went to see Ben's newest horse. Instead of jumping on its back right away, as Ben did, Rosie spent time grooming its coat and talking in a soothing voice. Soon, she and the horse were friends. When Ben arrived, Rosie was trotting around the stable yard on its back.

"Rosie," cried Ben, "you're amazing!"

"So, can I can ride your horse too?" Rosie asked.

Ben laughed. "Yes, and I'll clean out the stalls today. I want to watch you and learn some tips!"

The Key of the Kingdom

This is the key of the kingdom:
In that kingdom is a city,
In that city is a town,
In that town there is a street,
In that street there winds a lane,
In that lane there is a yard,
In that yard there is a house,
In that house there waits a room,
In that room there is a bed,
On that bed there is a basket,
A basket of flowers.

Flowers in the basket,
Basket on the bed,
Bed in the chamber,
Chamber in the house,
House in the weedy yard,
Yard in the winding lane,
Lane in the broad street,
Street in the high town,
Town in the city,
City in the kingdom:
This is the key of the kingdom.
Of the kingdom this is the key.

Bertha Saves the Day

Bertha Bunny had a shiny nose,
But this she could not mend,
Because her little powder puff
Was at the other end!

One day, the bunnies hopped and skipped
And wandered off to play
Too far into the Wicked Wood,
Then couldn't find their way!

It got so dark, they couldn't tell
Just which way they should go.
Then Bertie spotted Bertha's nose,
All shiny and aglow!

"Bertha's nose will light our way!"
Cried Bertie Bun with glee.
"Yippeeee!" the other bunnies yelled.
"We'll soon be home for tea!"

Index

383